THE ELF'S PRINCE

MISMATCHED PRINCES BOOK TWO

SIENNA SWAY

THE ELF'S PRINCE

MISMATCHED PRINCES BOOK TWO

SIENNA SWAY

THE
OAF
HOLD

CASETRO

SUVAHL

THE
ELVEN
VEIL

TASNIA

SEASHELL
ISLES

SENNA

HUNDAR

N

The Elf's Prince

A novel by

Sienna Sway

Published by

Blue Crescent Books

978-1-990307-02-7

CONTENTS

CHAPTER 1

ALLARD

*P*rince Allard stared out at the horizon, watching the sun slowly set.

For months now the extent of his entertainment had been watching the sunrise and fall over the kingdom. Sometimes he sat by his bedroom window, sometimes he watched from the garden.

He hadn't gone hunting. He hadn't practiced with his sword. He hadn't gone to *any* of the parties.

Quite frankly, he was moping.

He would very much appreciate being left to his moping too, but his mother, in particular, was quite sick of it.

Allard sighed and grudgingly pushed to his feet.

His manservant, Sten, was waiting patiently to

dress him. The serious man never so much as remarked on anything Allard said or did. He didn't need to. Now that the world had been flipped upside down for the prince, he could see quite clearly how silly he had always been. *Ridiculous*, in fact.

Prince Allard had only ever known being the center of attention. He'd fed on it all these years, showing off whenever he could. He adored adoration.

Then the other prince and princess had arrived from Suvahl and turned everything on its head.

He'd been so used to the rules he'd been raised with that he had never questioned them; everything *not* human was a lesser being, men were strong and masculine, women were soft and demure.

But then, the oves had been more likable than Allard had expected and Desada had been a better hunter than any of the men he knew and Nemir…

Allard sighed and held out his arms, remaining deep in his thoughts while he was dressed. Prince Nemir had been uptight, nervous, a little rude, and… *fascinating* to Allard. Only when he had been kidnapped and forced into a marriage with an oaf had the truth of Allard's feelings become clear to him.

How ironic that Allard, the most eligible bachelor, the one that women fawned over, should be more interested in men.

"Do you approve?" Sten asked, finally drawing Allard from his thoughts.

He looked at himself in the mirror before him, surprised to realize that he was already decked head to toe in a luxurious white suit laden with gold and blue accents.

Though this was meant to be a grand ball, one of the biggest of the year, according to his mother, with dignitaries and royalty from far and wide in attendance as well as other, *very special* guests—whatever that meant, Allard had no desire to make an appearance.

But make an appearance he would. He looked good. The golden light of the sunset through the window lit his pale hair on fire. His angular jaw was set and eyes, already a stormy grey, appeared to be more turbulent than ever.

"I look amazing," he sighed.

Sten's lips twitched but he did not respond otherwise.

Allard took his time going, even though he was ready, stalling as long as he could. Music led him to the party where the guests had already arrived by the time he finally entered the ballroom.

There was the usual stir of interest that a prince

entering a room always generated when he did. Allard allowed the moment, pretending he didn't notice as he took in the room. It was elegantly decorated with red flowers and gold-laden tables. In strategic places, rich red fabrics draped, like around the stage where the orchestra played a sweeping tune, perfect for spinning a partner.

Indeed, the dance floor was full of couples.

Prince Allard loved to dance, perhaps a few numbers and a drink or two wouldn't be so bad.

Across the hall, his father caught his eye and gestured for him. Allard moved to join him at once and suddenly stopped.

His father was in mid-conversation with someone who was pointedly *not* human—and it wasn't just the pointed ears that made him think so. The man was slender and ethereal, with long green hair that shone in the lights.

And that was when Allard realized just how different this party was.

All around him, various human-like beings mingled. Some of them wore their own cultural dress, like the elves, in richly decorated robes. Others towered over the rest of the guests.

Shocked, Prince Allard realized that there were *oves* here. In his home.

Yes, they were at peace now. Yes, Allard had

made friends with some of them, but that wasn't the point.

It was hard to imagine the oves anywhere but in the wilderness, where they lived. Yet here they were, at a ball, and the image was jarring, just like it had been at Prince Nemir's wedding.

Someone caught his eye, a young lady, eager to make his acquaintance. Prince Allard was already in the wrong state of mind to be pandered to—and then the girl's eyes caught the light, glinting unnaturally.

Allard shivered and stumbled back.

"Oof, careful there, friend."

Hands clasped his shoulders, steadying him and Allard glanced over, relieved to see a familiar face.

"Prince Nikolai! You're here too?"

"Of course! Everyone is!" His friend patted his shoulder with his usual enthusiasm. "What a revolutionary moment! I commend you and your family for choosing to bring the creatures of the wood to light. Such a daring idea."

His dark eyes twinkled with excitement and Allard couldn't bring himself to ruin the mood.

"Uh... yes."

He looked around again, the horror he'd felt turning into something else entirely. *Anger.* How could *this* be considered a good idea?

"Have you met Soren? He's an actual shape-shifter!"

Before Allard could even follow his friend's excited gestures at the man, a delicate hand landed on his elbow.

With relief, Allard turned to find his mother giving him a glowing smile.

"There you are dear, I was looking for you."

"I was about to do the same," Allard informed her. "May we speak in private?"

Although her expression bellied no awareness of his mood, they knew each other well enough that Allard could sense the shift in her.

"Of course."

He waved to Prince Nikolai as she led him quietly from the hall into one of the adjoining chambers. It happened to be empty but for the manservant preparing more trays of wine glasses to be distributed.

"What is it now?" Queen Barnett asked, dropping the serene act.

"What do you think?!" Allard demanded. "How could you throw a party like this without at least consulting me, or letting me know? What were you and father thinking?"

She gave him a very indulgent look and shook her head.

"Allard dear, you've been so distracted lately. I told you the details at least ten times myself."

Allard blinked.

"Really?"

She nodded.

"Yes, of course. We've been planning this for months. Due to Prince Nemir's influence, the oves were open to joining. The shifters took some time to even track down, but the elves proved to be the most resistant." She shrugged. "In the end, many different humanoid species chose to come. Isn't that lovely?"

She came forward and lightly dusted Allard's shoulders as though any dust could be on his impeccable clothing and then shook her head.

"I know that whole ordeal was difficult for you," she said and before Allard could so much as shake his head, she went on. "I know you like to be the hero and there was nothing you could do in the end, but it's time to put all that behind you."

Prince Allard swallowed.

"But to invite them into our home..."

"We used to be at war with the oves," Queen Barnett reminded him. "Now, due to Prince Nemir's fortuitous joining of one of *our* subjects, there is peace and we have a new ally. There's nothing wrong with that, now is there?"

"Yes, but," Prince Allard lowered his voice.

"Prince Nemir was *forced* into that union... I know it somehow turned into a happy ending, but do you support a joining of that... nature?"

Suddenly, his heart raced because the question was out and it didn't *just* apply to prince Nemir, and it didn't *just* apply to the differences in their species. Nemir and Soluc were both men. Would his mother gather his meaning?

She shrugged a shoulder lightly.

"Well, he's not *my* son," she laughed. "If the Suvahl royal family accepts their union, then why should *we* argue?"

Prince Allard's stomach twisted.

"Come now, your father has important business to discuss with you."

Allard allowed himself to be led from the room, back into the energetic festivities that immediately overwhelmed him and set him on edge.

He tried to pull it together, to focus on only the facts and not his mother's dismissive words, as he was led to his father where he still stood in discussion with the elf that had first startled him.

"Ah, at last," King Jareth said, making room for Allard to join them on the crowded floor. "This is my son, Prince Allard."

The elf, even more flawless up close, did not offer his hand but nodded to Allard instead.

"I am Seneca," he said. "Of the elven court."

Allard didn't know what that meant. The elven structure system was clearly different to the human's, but did the courts rule? Was this the king, or some sort of royalty, at least? He returned the nod, hoping that was enough.

"Seneca was just telling me of the elven woods and valleys, such a fascinating culture right at our doorsteps."

"Indeed," Allard said.

"We would like to send you to tour their land," his father said, "and strengthen our bond. See that their needs are all met."

"We are well equipped," the elf replied benignly, "but you are welcome to join me on my return home."

Stunned, Allard looked between the two.

"It will be something fun for you to do."

His father winked at him.

Allard fought for something to say. He didn't feel like doing anything lately. He wanted to stay home… which was probably exactly the reason his father wanted him to go.

"I'm sure your land is lovely," he began.

He would have added more, but just at that moment, he caught sight of someone whose sudden appearance gave him a most unpleasant stab in the chest.

Nemir was here. As lovely as ever, the other prince had his dark curls pulled back to expose his features and he looked so happy, glowing, even, despite the fact that he was holding onto the large arm of his spouse.

In Allard's opinion, the oaf Soluc favored the ogre side of his blood over the elf side. He was massive, towering over a foot taller than Nemir. His large frame was brutish, even in human clothes, with his hair tied up in an intricate design.

Yet they looked so happy together.

How?

For the millionth time, Allard found himself wondering how they could love each other so much and be so different.

And he would sit and brood and wonder that over and over for the next year if he let himself.

"I would love to go," Allard said.

CHAPTER 2

ALLARD

*A*llard woke with a splitting headache, still in his rumpled ball clothes. A *very* disgruntled Sten standing over his bed.

"Sire," he said, emphasizing the word, as though he'd been repeating it over and over. "You must rise. There is not much time left."

"Time?" Allard asked. "For what?"

After months spent lounging around at home, it was hard for his sluggish brain to wrap around the idea of rushing to do anything.

"You will be leaving soon," Sten reminded him. Then, when Allard only blinked at him, he went on. "For the elven land."

It all came rushing back to him then and Allard sat up suddenly—and instantly regretted it.

He reached out for something steady to hold onto, gripping Sten by the arm and hoping the older man was sturdy enough to stop the world from spinning.

"Oh goodness," he groaned.

"Release me," Sten said.

Allard did at once, gripping the bed instead.

"I apologize," he muttered. "Everything is spinning."

"I only wanted to get these for you," Sten said kindly, suddenly offering Allard a large glass of water and a small glass of the disgusting hangover remedy that the palace doctor made. Allard recognized the putrid smell. He still was only half sure that the doctor did not simply wipe his own arse down with a wet cloth and then ring it into a glass. It was the most disgusting thing Allard had ever ingested.

The last time he'd taken it, he'd sworn profusely that he never would again, especially since it didn't work at all.

But he was in incredible discomfort now. His body was trembling, muscles sore, stomach-churning, and head aching. There was no way he could get anywhere but to a bucket to puke in, let alone to the elven land. A carriage ride would kill him.

With a deep breath, Allard grabbed the small glass and downed the concoction, much the same way he had been downing shots all night at the ball.

A shudder ran through him, and he started to choke. The disgusting liquid wouldn't stay down.

Gagging, Allard jumped to his feet, desperate to get to the chamber pot before the contents of his stomach upended. He didn't make it far though considering that the room was still whipping around him.

He fell to his knees but before the inevitable vomiting began, a bowl was thrust under his face.

Allard retched, the disgusting doctor's remedy coming out first, momentarily followed by bile and alcohol from the night before.

Eventually, he collapsed on his side on the floor.

"Why did I do this to myself?" he groaned.

Sten's voice came from somewhere above him.

"Not sure, my lord. I thought your body was a temple?"

"When did I ever say anything so ridiculous?"

"The last time was just yesterday afternoon, I believe."

Allard would have grumbled at his manservant but his stomach was churning again.

"The bucket!"

It was promptly placed under his face, just before the carpet was subjected to the consequences of his reckless drinking.

"Get it all out," Sten said in his cool, soothing voice. "It's better for your body."

"Is that why that shite is so disgusting?" Allard demanded. "To forcibly make one remove the alcohol from their system?"

"Perhaps you should ask Doctor Thwain."

Allard sighed and rolled onto his back. Surprisingly, after a minute, he was starting to feel a little bit better. The room wasn't quite as unstable, and his stomach wasn't eager to be emptied. His head still throbbed, but that pain was more bearable in his opinion.

Why had he indulged to such a level? It wasn't like him. In fact, Allard didn't ever drink more than a glass of wine at dinner. He liked to have his full mental capacity. He liked to dance well at balls and flirt with the women he danced with—even though he had never had any intention of doing any more than that. which made sense, now that he was fully aware that he was not interested in women in that way... which was probably why he had buried himself in a bottle of wine, or two.

Allard distinctly remembered having to get

halfway through a bottle before he was able to go talk to his former crush, Nemir. That hadn't stopped the other man from being adorably tempting.

"Too bad he was there with his husband," Allard sighed.

"What was that?" Sten asked.

Allard opened his eyes blearily.

"Oh, nothing. I forgot you were here."

"I'm used to that," Sten said. Then he came to Allard, the dirty bowl already moved elsewhere, and helped him carefully to his feet.

"Come now, a hot bath, followed by coffee and toast will fix you right up."

Allard allowed himself to be steered to his washroom, where the large tub was already filled with soapy water.

The sight of himself in the mirror was enough to make him shudder, so he turned away from it and stood still while he was undressed.

"Would you like my assistance?" Sten asked as Allard climbed into the tub.

He shook his head and sank into the water, grateful to be alone by the time he settled into its comforting warmth.

By the time Allard got out and wrapped himself in a robe, breakfast was sitting on the table by his bed.

As promised, a strong coffee sat next to plain toast which he ate gratefully.

When he emerged from his room, clean and dressed, he was almost feeling like himself again.

His mother and father were both waiting for him in the entry hall.

He approached them with a regretful smile that he couldn't quite hold down. Allard hated the idea of his parents seeing him lose control the way he had last night. But if he'd made a fool of himself, this time neither one mentioned it.

Instead, his mother came and took both of his hands in her gloved fingers and looked up into his eyes.

"I'm so glad you decided to go," she said. "Have a lovely time with the elves, dear."

"Be cordial and understanding of their ways," his father added, his voice stern. "We are trying to make allies, not enemies."

"What exactly do you expect me to do?" Allard asked, tersely.

"After last night, I'm sure I don't know what to expect."

Ah. There it was.

Allard's cheeks heated.

He didn't have an appropriate argument. He barely remembered most of the night.

"I apologize if I embarrassed you," he managed to say, but then couldn't help adding, "but it was you who sprung that ball on me with no warning--"

"No warning?!"

His bellow echoed through the empty hall.

"Enough now," his mother cut in. "Let's not end our goodbye with an argument."

She turned her gaze to Allard, gray eyes so like his own, reproachful.

"Dear, I told you all about what happened last night. You've been too distracted lately. Oh well, it all worked out in the end."

The door swung open then, morning light spilling across the marble floors, silhouetting one of the footmen.

"The horses are ready, your highnesses," he informed them. "The elves are mounting to take their leave."

"We're going on horseback?" Allard asked, surprised.

"The carriages cannot go through the forest off the path," King Jareth spat. "Use your head boy. Or else, at least come back with a new one."

"Jareth!" his mother said, appalled, but his father was in a mood, unperturbed by his wife's disapproval. "We've tried to be patient, but this is the end of your moping. You come back from this trip

17

sharpened and ready to be a part of this family and this monarchy or there will be consequences."

Allard's jaw clenched.

Without a backward glance, ignoring even his mother's please, he marched outside.

The sun made him wince, his head still hadn't entirely recovered, but stubbornness made him press on as though it didn't bother him.

Allard could see the horses, already ready to depart. Some had riders already, others were still waiting.

He spotted one of the stable hands and went to him, stroking his mare's shoulder in greeting.

"Hello Blossom," he said to her, immediately soothed by her steady presence, even as more elves arrived around him.

"She's ready to go," the stable boy told him, strapping his bag to the saddle. Allard nodded and thanked him, then watched him go, regretfully. He looked around at the departing party. Twelve others were traveling with him. All elves.

His stomach squeezed with unease.

Allard couldn't help distrusting them. He didn't know anything about elves, only that they had a culture very different from his own. They were hard to read, the few times he had met them. This time was no exception.

All took turns looking at him and he nodded politely to each. They did the same, but no one spoke. Even the girl whom he remembered he had danced with last night, was now silent, watching him with large, interested eyes.

He climbed atop Blossom, and looked ahead, awkwardly awaiting *something*.

Finally, he realized that one of the horses was missing its rider. That's what they must be waiting for. A glance around told him that Seneca was the one missing and sure enough, when he looked back, his father was walking with the elf, chatting amicably. Clearly, their argument hadn't bothered him as much as it had bothered Allard.

He watched, wondering if they were talking about him. They bowed politely to one another and then, his father turned back to the palace and Seneca continued to his horse.

When he reached the white stallion and climbed atop him, he looked at Allard and offered him a smile.

"We're glad to have you join us," he said. "The council will be grateful to get to know our human prince."

With that, he kicked forward, the rest of them falling into line behind him.

The awkwardness he felt continued as they rode

past the palace gates, through the town, where they were gawked at.

Familiar people waved at him. Normally, he stopped and spoke to the townspeople when he was passing through, but in this case, with the elves' cold, curious gazes on them, Allard felt uncomfortable even waving back. They were so subdued that he was sure if he were to say *hello*, he may as well have been jumping up and down shouting, according to them.

Once they cleared the human villages, which were mostly clustered around the palace, their pace quickened.

It was impressive, really. They seemed to move as a unit, not needing to speak. When one hurried, the rest did as well.

Allard fell in line at the back, which made it easier for him to follow without breaking their practiced rhythm.

Ahead of them, the Green Veil loomed. From a distance, the thick line of forest that stretched across Tasnia and ran into the kingdom of Casetro looked like an impenetrable wall of darkness and green. Allard knew otherwise, of course.

For many years, he had prided himself in his hunting ability. Going into the forest alone and returning home with big game had almost been a right of passage. Now, as he had come to question so many things in his life that he hadn't analyzed before, he wondered if he had needed to prove something.

His masculinity, perhaps.

The thought made him shake his head.

He'd been unbearably out of touch with his true self, hadn't he? How had anyone been able to bear him?

Either way, he had built an understanding of the Green Veil. It was a dense wilderness that was not safe for most. In its depths, were a multitude of creatures that had until now, been better avoided. But things changed, and now Allard went willingly into the homes of one such species.

They slowed when they entered the forest. Initially, they took one of the narrow paths, the day plunging into shadow as they did, but eventually, Seneca, who was at the front of the procession, turned off the path, straight into the trees.

Allard's heart pumped as he followed him. He had not often gone off path unless necessary and that was usually just to retrieve his fallen prize. He never went in far. The only time he had, had been to rescue Prince Nemir, who, it turned out, did not need his rescuing.

Surprisingly, they never came to a dead-end,

never had to find another course. If there was a path ahead of them, Allard didn't see it, but the others rode with confidence as though there was one. Perhaps they simply knew the forest that well. Well enough to avoid the swamps and ogres' traps and all the other dangerous creatures that lurked.

It was a comforting thought and some of the tension eased from Allard's shoulders.

Hours passed with no discussion or signs of stopping for rest or food. Allard sipped from his water bottle to ease his cramping stomach. It still wasn't feeling very strong. Food was probably best avoided anyway.

Allard wasn't expecting the elven land to so suddenly surround them. When it did, it was like stepping through a gateway of trees and suddenly appearing in another world.

The trees here were just as large as the rest of the forest, but the areas around them had been cleared. Intricate stonework tiled the ground. Above, buildings glistened, worked into the trees with winding staircases in mazes above his head, shimmering lights were strung through the leaves, giving the whole place an ethereal glow.

Breathless, Allard dismounted, his jaw agape as he turned slowly to take it all in. Everywhere he looked, something new and astounding caught his eyes.

"Are you impressed?" Seneca asked, coming to stand next to him.

Allard managed to shut his mouth but nodded.

"This is incredible," he said.

Seneca smiled.

"I'm glad you appreciate our city. You are the first human I know of who has been allowed to enter."

Allard gulped, suddenly moved that he had been invited.

"I appreciate that greatly," he said. "I wasn't sure what to expect. I knew you lived in the Green Veil, but that was all I knew."

"Likewise, we elves knew of the human towns and palaces. To see it in the flesh, to get a sense of your culture and energy as a species was truly fascinating."

Allard smiled, warmth filling him. Perhaps this trip was a good idea after all.

"Come, I'm sure you are eager to recharge."

Allard glanced around. The others had already dispersed, some riding their horses, others walking them away.

There were elves on the streets, some in the trees above, but the whole place was oddly quiet.

A human town would never be so peaceful.

"What about my horse?" he asked, but even as he did, another elf arrived, taking his and Seneca's by the reigns with a nod toward them both.

"They will be cared for in the stables," Seneca informed him, turning, expecting Allard to follow.

He did, falling into step just behind the elf.

Seneca's pale green hair glistened and swayed as he walked, and Allard's gaze was drawn to it. Surrounded by the mysterious Green Veil, in the very kingdom of the elves, their unique coloring seemed more natural than Allard's own golden locks. Their ethereal appearance fit their setting. Allard probably stood out, plain and unpolished by comparison. A frisson of self-doubt hit him. Great. The one thing Allard had never doubted before; his physical appearance, was now the next thing on the list to scrutinize about himself.

He pushed the feeling down and continued.

Seneca led him down a long street. On one side, there was a row of what appeared to be shops, weaponry displayed in the windows of one, jewelry in another, fabrics in the next. It was all so luxurious. He would have to take some of the blue fabrics to his seamstress. The shops didn't hold his attention long though, when he realized that on the other side of the narrow walkway, past a thin, intricate railing, there was a massive drop. The cavernous hole went deep with walkways and buildings and bridges in all directions.

Once again, Allard was blown away.

He shook his head, steps slowing as he took in the incredible sight.

"This way," Seneca said.

Allard looked over to find Seneca had already turned down another street, away from the center that Allard was so in awe of. Hastily, he went after the elf, surprised when he was led back to what appeared to be the outskirts of the city. The wilderness once again thickened around them, but he continued until they reached another clearing with a pool in the center. The water had a faint glow, a gentle steam rose from all around it. On the sides, benches sat, shrouded in bushes.

"I have business to attend to with the council," Seneca informed him. "You will be taken care of in the meantime."

"Oh," Allard said, looking around, startled. "Do you want me to remain here?"

He was a little taken aback, but the elf only smiled at him benignly.

"Please do not take offense," he said. "You seem worse for wear today. The healing pools are a treasure of Elven Veil. The water will restore you to your top form. You may relax here until you are called for."

He waited until Allard nodded and then departed, just like that.

For a moment, Allard stood in the clearing, unsure what to do. Eventually, he peeled off the layers of his riding clothes, wondering where his bags had gotten to, and tiptoed into the shallow pool.

The water was warm and immediately soothing, just like Seneca said it would be. When he stood, it only came to his waist, but a seat had been set around the edge which brought the water to his chest when he settled into it.

He wasn't sure he felt himself healing but after a few minutes, his body felt stronger, more invigorated. His mind sharpened like he'd had a cup of coffee and a cold glass of water at the same time.

When his headache eased, he finally believed Seneca's words. Impressed, despite himself, he wondered how extensive an injury these waters could remedy.

In a very short time, Allard was already in awe of the Elven Veil. They had a beautiful home here; one any human would ache to see in person. And the elves themselves, all seemed to be like their land; beautiful, intricate, deep, and elusive.

The longer Allard sat in the warm waters, waiting for someone to come to him, the more his thoughts were confirmed.

The elves were cold compared to humans and even their brother species, oves. At the very least, Allard would have expected to be given some company.

The quiet of the woods was overwhelming. What he had thought of as peaceful was now oppressively silent. What was supposed to soothe him, now made Allard feel utterly alone.

Suddenly, he just wanted to go home… but this trip was supposed to be his escape from that. It seemed there was nowhere for Allard to go where he wouldn't feel so completely unwanted.

CHAPTER 3

SENECA

*A*fter the utter chaos that was humanity, Seneca was blissfully content to be in the quiet of the woods, his home, Elven Veil.

He took his seat next to the other council members, elves he had known for longer than he could count. Despite the unpleasantness that was about to unfold, his spirit was soothed by their presence.

"Seneca," Yana said, "welcome home."

"Thank you," he smiled. "I'm glad to be back."

"So, the human festivities were less enjoyable than anticipated?"

"Oh no, they were exactly what I expected.

Except of course, for the human prince, I returned with."

"I never took you for the type to consort with humans," Nelis said curiously. Seneca smiled.

"I didn't bring him home for my own enjoyment. I promised the human king to show him our culture. They're eager to make connections in this current political climate."

"I still don't know why you would bother. We don't need them as allies."

Seneca looked at Elli, she was ever the cynic among them.

"We are technically within their land."

"In their territory, yes, but they do not own the Elven Veil," Kial argued. "If they threatened us for it, they would meet their ends."

"Before they even knew we were there," Seneca agreed, ever proud of the elves he commanded. "Still, it's better to have friends than enemies. They invited us into their home, returning the gesture does us no harm."

"What are the humans like?" Elli asked.

"Loud," Seneca said and left it at that while the others chuckled.

"I would love to meet the prince," Yana said, "but for now, we should prepare ourselves for *Fenian*."

"What is there to prepare ourselves for?" Kial demanded. "This appeal is a waste of our time. His actions deserve the consequences he now faces."

"He disagrees."

"His opinion doesn't matter. Ours do, and mine will not be swayed."

"Still," Nellis interjected. "He deserves to argue his side. That is our law."

Not knowing who was listening, Seneca silently sent the words directly into their minds so they would not be overheard.

I can only imagine how hard he would argue if he knew the truth.

"You sound as though you are second-guessing our decision," Elli said, watching him closely.

Seneca smiled tersely.

"I will not fight the group. You have my support."

Just then, as one, they sensed movement and turned to look at the path.

Through the trees, Seneca caught glimpses of the forest green of the guards' uniforms. They were approaching, the prisoner in tow.

Seneca's mood turned suddenly dark. If that small child Seneca had known had turned down a different path, if he had not been so stubborn and troublesome, things would be different.

He didn't know who to blame.

* * *

FENIAN

THE GUARDS PUSHED Fenian's shoulders down as one.

Gritting his teeth, he slowly gave in to the pressure, forcing his knees to bend, his head to bow. In this position, the cold metal of the handcuffs cut mercilessly into his wrists.

A long silence met Fenian's submission. He waited, anger boiling as he did. His lip was twisted in a snarl that he could barely contain.

He was finally before the council. After having to nearly beg for his right to an appeal, he was here, and all he wanted to do was destroy the group of elders who had put him in this position, to begin with.

He took a long, slow breath, trying to clear his mind, trying to remember that his *life* was worth more than the satisfaction he would get from fighting with the council.

Dawnya have you come to regret your choices?

A sharp intake of breath was Fenian's only response to the silent question. He recognized Yana's voice, especially whispered in his mind. She was the oldest on the council, perhaps that was why she gave Fenian the childlike endearment. Dawnya meant naive, immature, perhaps even innocent. Was that how she thought of Fenian?

Swallowing, he risked a glance up.

Just like when he'd arrived, the five members of the council were seated before him, expressions neutral. Yana, of course, Elli, Nelis, Kial, and Seneca. Each was older than Fenian knew and had more of a superiority complex than anyone else could possibly have. Still, he withheld his irritation and met Yana's icy blue eyes.

"If you really think of me as someone to be addressed as *Dawnya*, surely my execution is unfair."

He would play along if he had to, especially if it would save him.

Yana exchanged a look with the others and Fenian's heart leaped with hope. Council decisions were rarely changed but perhaps in this case...

"I am young. I am still learning. It was a mistake—"

"Your mistake cost someone their life," Seneca cut in.

"A family has been torn apart," Elli said and Kial went on. "Your continued disregard for order, safety, and the law is reprehensible."

"It is irreversible," Nelis finished.

They spoke so cohesively, so much like they were one being that Fenian was sure they were speaking to one another silently. Conversing in front of him in a way he could not hear.

He took a slow breath.

"I know Sabina's death is irreversible—"

"No," Yana interrupted. "Although your actions cannot be undone. We are addressing your appeal. The order is irreversible. Your execution will be held tomorrow morning, as scheduled."

"There will be no further discussion on the matter. I must go. I have the human prince to attend to," Seneca added, and as one, they stood.

Fenian stared, his eyes widening, heart racing.

That couldn't be it. Entertaining some human prince was more important than his life?

Then, why even see me? he demanded silently.

Because Dawna, Yana replied, *that is our way.*

Our way… Fenian wanted to laugh, shout, or *run.*

The second the thought was in his head, just as he was lifted roughly to his feet to be taken back to his chilly cell, Fenian knew it was his only option.

Without thinking, his head flew back, skull cracking into a nose with such force it nearly knocked him off his feet.

The guard stumbled back, shocked, blood flying

through the air, and then all Fenian had to do was go.

He took off, rolling out of the other guard's hands that hastily grabbed at him, and then suddenly, he was free!

He ran, desperation pushing him. In a few long strides, he was out of the council's courtroom. People were shouting behind him, but he didn't dare look back.

Don't be so ridiculous, Seneca's voice entered his mind. *There is nowhere you can run.*

He was right of course, but that didn't stop Fenian from trying. He broke into the main city, boots hitting the polished stones as he ran. Behind him, people started shouting to stop him.

Fenian's heart was hitting his ribs like a drum, his breaths were coming in ragged gasps, his wrists in agony from the cuffs, blood now warming his back where they were pressed.

He was an obvious convict in the blue uniform, literally on the run with no plan whatsoever but if he stopped and let them catch him, he would be dead in the morning. He had to at least *try*.

"Stop him!"

Ahead, people were turning to see what the commotion was. He could see the shocked faces of the people he whipped past, hoping that no one got involved.

To his right was the drop to the city center, but if he went forward, he could veer into the wilderness. He was so close.

An arrow whizzed past his ear and Fenian stumbled.

He caught himself at the last second, but then another arrow came, and another.

He stumbled, tripped, and hit the small railing. The thin decorative metal was the only thing to keep one from falling into the depths of the city, many stories below. If he'd had his hands free, he could have stopped himself from going over. As it was, it seemed that his life was going to end even earlier than the others had planned.

Fenian didn't scream as he fell, he couldn't. His breath caught in his throat, and he simply dropped, but not as far as he'd thought he would.

Just as quickly as he fell, he hit something, then fell *through* it, and then landed in an explosion of dust, and shocked shouts.

For a minute, probably more, Fenian lay where he was, eyes closed, gasping in the strange, dusty air, overwhelmingly grateful to still be alive.

His body was aching. He could not tell how badly he had been hurt. The sharpest pain was in his shoulder and hip but after a moment it started to dull. Somehow, he was okay. He remained completely still, eyes closed, body shaking with adrenaline as he tried to regain composure. For a moment there, he'd really thought it was all over.

When he finally opened his eyes, he found that he was in a dark storeroom. There were shelves across from him with countless jars and baskets, all filled with what appeared to be powder. Above him, a hole in the ceiling cast him in a weak spotlight.

The pit into the city center had walkways all the way down. Most were narrow, but certain areas were wide enough to squeeze small shops or storerooms, tucked against the cliffside. How he had been lucky enough to land where there was one to break his fall, he had no idea. If not for his current predicament, he would have considered himself lucky.

Suddenly, the door before him swung open. To Fenian's disgust, it wasn't simply the guards who had come to retrieve him. The entire council stood before him, varying degrees of anger in their expressions. Somehow, that mollified him a little bit. At least it wasn't just Fenian who was suffering.

They stepped inside the room, guards following and gripping him by the arms, yanking him unsympathetically up from the pile of baskets and shelves and broken glass he was lying in.

"That was a foolish thing to do," Yana repri-manded. "Luckily you landed here. You could have killed someone."

Fenian grinned.

"I only seem to do foolish things, don't I? The least I can do is remain true to character until the very end."

"You've wasted months of spell supplies," Elli said coldly, as though that was just as bad.

"Take him to his cell," Kial ordered.

Fenian didn't fight it this time. There was nowhere for him to run to, and his body was now screaming as he was half-dragged away. His hip burned every time he put weight on it. Nerves thrummed with pain all over his upper back. Even if he tried to get away once more, he wouldn't get far.

Still, it was with the taste of bile rising in his throat that Fenian allowed himself to be pushed back into his cell. He stumbled but managed to catch himself before falling, panic rising as they locked his cell.

"Hey!" he shouted as they turned to walk away. "My wrists!"

Without waiting, he turned, pressing his hands against the cold bars. When he glanced over his shoulder, one of them begrudgingly came to him and undid his handcuffs.

That at least was a bit of relief.

He cradled his wrists and went to the far wall, seeking the shadows, then sank down against the floor. The unforgiving stone was cold enough to offer some relief to his damaged body. The blood had already dried on his sleeves.

When he had first been brought to this cell, skin injured by burns, they had taken the time to heal him. Fenian doubted that they would bother today. He wouldn't be in pain long if they had their way.

Desperation filled him, just as strong as hopelessness. He didn't want to die. Not yet.

Yes, he was no good. He didn't argue that. But still... he wanted a chance for... something more.

Sighing, his head fell back, hitting the stone wall.

His eyelashes, normally dark blue, like his hair, were coated with dust. It was in the folds of his shirt, inside his boots...

Fenian bolted upright, hissing in pain and having to still before he could properly think.

Spell dust.

The elves were proud of their dust, even though it could be made just as well by the oves and *they* could barely even light a fire. Either way, it was precious and Fenian was covered in it. A lot of it was mixed together, but he knew his magic well. If he could separate some of it, maybe it could be of use to him.

Fenian stood and walked to the bars, looking out.

There were guards on duty, as usual, but the afternoon was quiet, as it always was.

Silently, Fenian returned to his dark corner and began the careful process of meticulously separating the dust while he hid behind his bed.

He started with his boots, emptying them and sifting through what had spilled. It amounted to a handful of sand mixed.

From his shirt, he shook loose a generous amount from the collar.

Everything else on him was too mixed up to bother with. Instead, he walked to the bars and dusted himself off, especially shaking out the long strands of his hair and then tying it back into a knot, so as not to contaminate the piles he'd collected.

Then he returned to his piles and when he was sure no one was looking, he cast a low light over them.

To his immense disappointment, there were only two colors.

From the pile from his shirt, there was a mix of purples. Those were medical. Possibly useful so that his last night would be comfortable, but that was all it would be good for.

The rest, that he'd taken from his boot, was a deep red.

Bonding spell dust. *Useless.*

Cursing, Fenian hit the pile, dispersing the disappointing red dust across the floor.

Unless an escape offered itself up to him on a platter, he was all out of ideas.

CHAPTER 4

ALLARD

*W*hen someone finally came to retrieve Allard, he was sitting on one of the benches, dressed in his riding clothes again.

"I'm here to show you to your room," the elf said.

Allard nodded and stood, following her through the trees, back toward the city, but not quite entering it. He was led down a cobbled street until they stopped before a small house.

"Enjoy your stay, Prince," she said, and then departed.

Allard entered the simple dwelling. Inside, he was grateful to find his belongings, at least, had been set atop the table. The room itself was simple and small, but beautiful. It consisted of a bed, a dresser, and a desk and chair. There were lovely, decorative carvings on all the furniture and above, half the roof was made of glass, allowing light to enter, vines and leaves visible above. The single door inside led to a small washroom and that was it.

So far, this was all so different, Allard was unsure what to make of it. He appreciated having his own space but he felt almost stifled. As soon as he could, he would ask if it would be a problem for him to explore. At the very least, he would prefer that to waiting around, unsure what he should do with himself.

At the very least, the pool had been nice. He felt a bit more like himself again, but unrest still gnawed inside him. Hopefully, someone would come to retrieve him soon, at the very least, for some food and hopefully also for a tour.

Deciding that must be it, he went through his bag, pulling out a different outfit to change into. It had felt strange to pull his riding clothes back over his clean, damp skin. The fabric still felt wet in places.

No sooner had he fastened the last button on his collar, than there was a knock at the door.

"Come in."

Allard was relieved to see Seneca open the door, entering with a kind smile.

"I apologize for keeping you waiting," he said. "There was a meeting that I was unable to miss, but aside from bearing witness to council proceedings early tomorrow morning, I have no other obligations for the next few days."

Relief swamped Allard. He'd been hoping that was the case.

"It isn't a problem," he assured him.

"Very well. You must be hungry. I would like to invite you to share a meal with the council."

A genuine smile lit Allard's face.

"I would love that," he said.

He quickly pulled on his boots, fastening the laces, aware of Seneca watching curiously. Allard glanced at the elf's soft looking sandals.

"Those look a little more practical," he said, gesturing to them as he straightened.

"For the city, yes," he agreed. "Thicker shoes are essential for the woods, but ours are not made as heavily as yours appear."

"Why is that?"

"It's much better for mobility and speed," Seneca explained as he led him outside.

They went back into the city that Allard had only glimpsed before.

He looked longingly up at the incredible sight of life above and then down the railing at the mysterious depths below.

"I would love to get a tour," he voiced. "It's incredible here."

"Of course. I will take you to see anything you wish."

They went under an archway made of hanging branches, moss, and more of those small little lights that Allard was sure were made of magic. They emerged on the other side, in what appeared to be a market.

It was a little bit livelier. Where the shops he'd seen before seemed more like workshops, these were more what Allard was used to. There were stands selling food and trinkets and even medicine. There were restaurants and what he assumed were pubs with patio seating spread out on the street. The horses all appeared to be roaming free, not tied anywhere in waiting.

Elves walked the market, shopping or talking. Even children ran about, playing much the same way that human ones would.

Allard was relieved to see the similarities. It made the elves feel more familiar, despite their differences.

"This way."

Seneca led him into one of the restaurants.

Despite being human and a prince, no one made a big deal at Allard's presence. He received nods in greeting and the occasional smile when he caught someone's eye, but no one spoke to him.

In fact, they didn't even speak to each other. Seneca didn't even acknowledge the staff, he simply led Allard past all the tables and through the back door.

It led to a private patio where a table sat. Four stern-looking elves were already seated around it.

One, a beautiful, white-haired elf, waved him over.

"Don't be shy, Prince Allard. Come sit."

He smiled, fishing for some of the charms he had once possessed, and took one of the free seats.

"I am Yana," she said. "This is Elli, Nelis and Kial."

"Thank you for having me."

"You're most welcome, child," she said.

Allard managed to school his surprise at being called a child by someone who didn't look much older than him.

"Are you surprised by the Elven Veil?" Elli asked. "Seneca confirmed that the human lifestyle is very different."

"Yes, it's much quieter," Allard agreed.

That statement made a chuckle run through the

room, surprising Allard. He hadn't really thought the elves were the type to laugh, probably *ever.*

"It did take a few hours for my ears to adjust to the volume at your party," Seneca said.

Allard grimaced.

"I can imagine. Did you enjoy yourself?"

Seneca nodded.

"It was fascinating," he said thoughtfully. "To see so many beings mingle under one roof is a rare sight."

"Tell me, what inspired you to hold such a ball?" Nelis asked.

Allard searched for a viable reason.

"Well, I'm sure you know of the marriage between Prince Nemir and Soluc of the oves. It inspired my parents to reach out to the other beings in our land to make amends and friendships."

Considering he hadn't even known the ball was going to happen, he hoped he sounded convincing.

The others didn't say anything, a look was exchanged between them.

"What is it?" Allard asked uneasily.

Taking pity on him, Seneca offered an answer.

"Historically, we prefer to keep a distance from the oves," he explained. "Their species leans heavily on their ogre ancestry."

For a moment, Allard didn't know what to say.

He had avoided his oaf friends for a few months while wallowing in his own emotions, but he couldn't help thinking of them now, wanting to defend them.

"I used to feel the same way," he said. "But after getting to know a few of them, I was surprised to learn they possess an unexpected depth."

"We met Soluc and Nemir just after they initially bonded," Seneca said, surprising Allard. "Then, of course, I met them again during the ball… They do seem to truly care for one another. Perhaps an oaf and human are similar."

He made the statement like it was meant to appease Allard, but there was an undercurrent to it. They didn't like the oves, they'd as much as said that… and humans and oves were the same?

Allard felt the tension returning to his body. Annoyance and anger filled him along with his father's echoed words to make friends, not enemies with the elves. He bit his cheek.

The only way to make them change their minds about humans would be to win them over.

Just then, the door opened and two elves entered carrying trays of food.

It was laid out on the table. The dishes were different and he had to watch how the others plated their servings to understand how to eat them.

Despite how hungry he was, he took his time eating. The food was flavourful, a rich vegetable stew with a grill of various meats and vegetables, coated in marinades and spices. He would have devoured it but was too aware of his image and reputation now that he knew that they didn't think much about humans, to begin with.

How unfortunate that Seneca had seen him so drunk the night before and hungover this morning. He had already made a bad first impression, probably confirming everything the elf already thought about humans.

"It is very peaceful here," he said, attempting to compliment the often oppressive silence and it seemed to work when he was given a couple of genuine smiles from the others. "I'm sure your people value that. I can't imagine anyone ever causing any trouble."

At that, he received another chuckle.

"We must confess," Yana said, "that the silence is due mostly to the *inner speak*."

"Inner speak?" Allard repeated.

"We elves can talk amongst ourselves silently, by sending the words to another's mind."

Allard stared, unable to play uninterested.

"Really? That's incredible."

"It is, I suppose," Elli said. "But to us it's normal.

It is only part of the magic that elves possess. There are many things that every elf can do."

"Start small lights and fires, sense changes in the environment as they are coming, create small forcefields…"

"Forcefields? Without any walls?"

He received an indulgent smile from the whole group and suddenly, his hard feelings about their views on humans eased a bit. In a way, they were right; humans *were* different. They must seem very simple when creating fires with your mind was a normal part of elven life. Perhaps no offense had been intended.

"The forcefields are not physical walls. They are more like intentions. It is how we keep unwanted visitors from entering elven land. That is why we are not overrun by forest creatures. They simply pass us by."

Allard was truly amazed.

"As for troublemakers," Seneca said, shaking his head as though perturbed. "We have some of those, just as any society does, but we deal with them promptly to keep the peace."

"Deal with them?" Allard asked, a chill running down his spine.

"Long prison sentences for repeat offenders, followed by strict community work," Seneca said.

"For serious crimes, we have no mercy. Execution is the only fair response."

Allard was shocked. Executions didn't seem very fair to him. It had been outlawed in human society even before his grandparents' time. How odd to think that in this one way, the elves were more barbaric than the humans.

"Would you like me to show you the prisons?" Seneca asked. "We can start your tour there tonight, then do the larger sections of the city starting tomorrow."

Surprised, Allard nodded.

"I would like very much to see it."

He was beyond curious.

The dungeons below the castle, where he lived, were dark and dank. They were filled with rats and were icy cold. He rarely entered them because they were so unpleasant and anyone who spent time within it rarely made a second trip. He genuinely couldn't imagine the elven prison. There was no way that it would be like the human one.

Sure enough, when Seneca later took him on a stroll to the prison hold, Allard didn't even realize when they were in it.

The path they were on didn't even change. It remained a beautiful walkway, with a garden on one side and buildings on the other. Evening settled around them and it wasn't until he noticed the guards, standing rigidly every twenty or so feet that he even noticed the cells.

They were lined up along the path, a long stretch of them going as far as he could see. They were in the open, each cell with stone walls to the back and sides with bars along the front and beds visible within.

Allard assumed that the fact that there was no privacy or fourth wall against the weather was the only true hardship of being imprisoned. That and the small space. He wouldn't *like* to be held within one of the cells, but compared to the dank holes of the cells he knew back home, these were downright luxurious.

And empty.

Allard held in a smile.

Despite their statements of having their fair share of troublemakers, Allard couldn't spot anyone within the cells.

Still, they continued their evening stroll. Along the way, Seneca told him tidbits of information. He explained when they had been built, how many prisoners they could hold, and so on and Allard even started to enjoy himself.

Toward the end of the row movement suddenly caught his eye from within.

Allard paused in his step, gaze searching the dark cell.

"Is there someone in that one?" he asked after a moment.

"No one you need to worry about," Seneca informed him. "No one that anyone will need to worry about come tomorrow morning."

Again, Allard shivered at the cold statement. A realization filled him, making him feel sick. Perhaps the cells were empty, not because they didn't see their fair share of rule-breakers, but because they were swiftly executed?

"I'm sure you can't wait to be rid of me, Seneca, oh *wise* one."

A bitter voice emerged from the darkness of the cell. It was deep, smooth, and *cold* as ice. Still, Allard could not see who was within.

"Tell me, is that the human prince?" he asked. "The one who is more important than my life?"

Seneca's lip twisted into a slight grimace before he relaxed his features once again into the calm mask he often wore.

"You had already thrown your life away before your appeal," he informed the prisoner calmly. "Therefore, *everyone's* life is now more important than your own."

He turned to Allard, whose mind and heart were

racing from the exchange.

"Come," Seneca said. "Let us leave Fenian to wallow for his last remaining hours."

Suddenly, before Allard could so much as blink, there was an explosion.

Light burst and a *boom* filled the air. In the silence of the Elven Veil and the dim of night, it was shocking to the system.

Allard flinched, backing away from the sound before he even knew what had happened.

He spun around, watching the plume of smoke and fire that billowed from somewhere in the distance. Not so far away that it could be ignored, but not immediately in their path.

"Wait here!" Seneca shouted.

Allard watched as he took off, calling for the guards nearby to follow.

He pressed a hand to his chest, taking a deep breath to calm his frayed nerves. He wasn't normally so easily startled but this place was so quiet it set him on edge. An explosion was the last thing he would have expected.

* * *

SENECA

THE MOMENT SENECA reached the explosives storehouse and saw the raging fire, a single name jumped to the front of his mind.

Fenian.

He couldn't be sure, of course. Fenian was too far away to be setting fires like these. Then again, he'd always suspected that the rogue elf's abilities went far beyond what he showed, that he kept his secrets guarded like precious treasures. Like they were his only true possessions, which, Seneca supposed, they were.

This particular spot had been cleared of trees and underbrush for just this reason. Stepping stones and birdbaths surrounded the area to make it less lifeless, but the fire had frightened any animals away.

Is anyone there? he called silently.

He waited for a response from the direction of the flames but silence met him. When he shut his eyes and felt for living presence in the area, he sensed people approaching—his guards, and a few small animals. They flittered into his consciousness; a rodent scurrying away, a rabbit burrowing, but there was nothing else.

If anyone had been in there, they were already dead.

Knowing they were coming, Seneca waited until

members of the elven guard appeared around the storehouse, materializing from the shadows.

The explosion had burst through one of the walls. Burning and sizzling bits of wood were sprinkled around the area, mingling with the dirt and cobblestones.

He inhaled slowly, and as one, the others followed his lead, hands rising, palms forward to face the fire.

Altogether, he told them. *Three, two, one.*

Seneca felt the thickening moisture in the air. He pressed against it with his palms until it felt almost like a wall and his hands started to get wet.

As one, they all took a step, and then another, pressing the water against the building.

Slowly, the reaching flames faltered. As though they were being smothered, they grew smaller, compressing into what was left of the building, sizzling as it did.

By the time they reached the broken, blackened wood, it was saturated, dripping water down their arms, and soaking their clothes.

"One more push!"

Seneca grunted with the effort of holding the water, forcing it onto the fire.

With one last burst of effort, boots slipping in the

mud, there was a sudden sputtering of smoke billowing into the air and then, blessed silence.

Seneca released his hold on the air, his arms exhausted, chest heaving.

The others backed off, all in similar states.

One of his main guards shook herself and walked into the remains, examining what was left.

"What happened here?" she asked. "I didn't see anyone approach, and yet, this was clearly arson. Who would do such a thing? It would have to be someone powerful."

"Yes," Seneca agreed, realizing how long he'd left the prince alone just outside Fenian's cell. "Someone with a motive."

Without explaining, he turned, practically running from the location, worry overcoming him.

This was no accident and there was only one elf he knew who enjoyed setting fires for his own gain.

CHAPTER 5

ALLARD

"*I* have never met a human before..." The soft, deep voice from within the cell was closer now and Allard spun around, realizing that he'd backed nearly to the bars that held the prisoner Fenian.

He could finally see the elf within, a masculine silhouette in the darkness.

He took a step back, just out of arm's reach as the elf came forward, emerging from the shadows. Midnight blue hair hung past broad shoulders, his shirt was undone, exposing the smooth skin of his muscular chest. Sharp, dark eyes met Allard's, and a dark smile touched his full, pink lips.

"Come to think of it, I've never met a prince, either."

Allard didn't speak but he stood, mesmerized, shocked by the way his heart skipped under Fenian's scrutiny. He didn't dare move.

"Tell me," Fenian whispered, resting his arms on the bars. "What does it feel like to be so *privileged?*"

Allard swallowed, and his jaw tightened. He knew when he was being toyed with.

"Tell me why I should bother talking to you, and maybe I will," he replied.

For a moment, Fenian looked surprised, and then his eyes glinted with amusement, an uneven smile lifted one side of his lips, and Allard's entire insides somersaulted.

"I was only playing," Fenian said and then he reached his arm out past the bars, holding out a long, elegant hand toward Allard. "Please, come closer. I won't do anything to you."

This was a prisoner. One who was about to be executed, probably for committing terrible crimes, but lord help him, Allard did as he asked.

The whole while, his mind screamed at him not to, but he couldn't help the sudden curiosity. What did Fenian want to do to him? He would probably die if he didn't find out.

As Allard stepped forward, Fenian's hand landed

softly on his chest, just over his pounding heart. For a moment, he left it there, his expression unreadable, and then, he stroked gently up the fabric.

"You're exactly what I would guess a prince would look like," he informed Allard, hand reaching the collar of his shirt. "Defined muscles but soft skin." His fingers touched Allard's neck, making him shiver. He continued, fingers moving up, thumb stroking Allard's jaw. "Strong features, but still beautiful." He touched Allard's lips next and his whole body reacted. Allard was cold and hot at the same time. His heart was beating so fast, he thought it might burst.

"Wide eyes, so innocent," Fenian went on, almost thoughtfully, seeming to take no notice of Allard's body's reaction to him, except for the way his gaze darkened as he watched him. "And this, *cliche* yellow hair."

He pressed his hand into Allard's locks, suddenly fisting the strands. He yanked him closer, suddenly pressing Allard's face to the cold metal bars. For a moment, Allard thought that he was being attacked.

He gasped, hands swinging out to catch him, gripping the bars, but instead of being hit, soft, demanding lips met his.

For a moment, Allard didn't know what to do. All he could manage was to stand completely still while his body felt like it was about to combust. Fenian didn't seem to care though, he didn't pull back. He kissed Allard like his life depended on it, sucking his lips into his mouth, biting them gently. Allard gasped, coming back to life, suddenly desperate to take part as his deepest fantasy became a reality.

A man was kissing him!

He tilted his head, silently cursing the bars that barely gave room for their faces to meet. When he thrust his tongue out, Fenian accepted it into his mouth with a groan, sucking it gently.

Allard gasped, breaking apart. He instantly regretted it. For a split second, they stared at each other. Then, fist still in his hair, Fenian pulled him back for more. His other hand reached through the bars now too, gripping Allard by the hip, pulling him closer.

The damn *bars.* Allard would pay any price to have them removed, *right now.* He wanted Fenian unlike he had ever wanted anyone.

Suddenly, Fenian pulled back, an agitated noise in the back of his throat as he suddenly backed away into the shadows of his cell. His eyes bore into Allard's, filled with regret until the shadows overtook him.

Before Allard could even fathom what had

happened, he heard footsteps approaching and understood, backing hastily away from Fenian's cell.

From the shadows, Seneca emerged and hurried toward him.

Allard was sure that Fenian was about to be punished for touching him and his entire heart seized for a moment because he couldn't let that happen. Not when he'd wanted it.

Seneca stopped before him, his scrutinizing gaze raking him from top to bottom.

Allard's cheeks heated. Seneca could tell what had happened, he was sure. The elves could speak into each other's minds, maybe they could read them too.

As though to prove his point, Seneca looked deeply into the cell that held Fenian.

"I apologize for leaving you here," he finally said. "Allow me to escort you back to your room. Our tour will have to wait."

"I understand," Allard managed, heart racing. Remembering the fire, he turned back to where it had been. Smoke still billowed into the night.

"Is everything okay?" he asked.

Seneca shook his head.

"Someone set the explosives storeroom on fire. Luckily, no one was hurt. If anyone had been near, another life could have been lost," Seneca said, gaze shooting to the cell again. "This way, your highness."

Allard nodded, gaze flying back to the dark cell he'd been so eager to climb into. If Fenian was watching him, he had no idea. He could see nothing beyond the first foot of the cell, where the light reached.

He should say goodbye or *something.* After all, was this not Fenian's last night on Earth?

A dark feeling settled into the pit of Allard's stomach. Regret and disgust and understanding. Perhaps that was the reason that Fenian had kissed him. It was his one last chance to experience something pleasant.

Seneca was already walking away, expecting him to follow.

"My name is Allard," he said quietly toward the cell. There was no movement inside, no sounds, no acknowledgment.

Allard hurried after Seneca.

The elf was only a few paces ahead, but he slowed so that Allard could reach him.

They walked in silence until they were a certain distance from the cells and then Seneca stopped abruptly and turned to him.

"Did he do or say anything to you?" he asked.

Allard's mouth went dry. His throat closed.

Seneca didn't know then. Relief flooded him at the same time that his mind went blank.

"…What?"

"The prisoner," Seneca said patiently. "Fenian. Did you have any interaction while I was not there?"

Allard shrugged helplessly.

"Well…"

Seneca's gaze was hard to take. His eyes, the unnaturally pale green reminded Allard of the wolves he sometimes saw when he was hunting. It was hard to look at him at all when he knew the elf saw more than Allard knew.

"What did he do?"

Allard shook his head.

"He mocked me."

"What did he say?"

"That—that I was privileged and spoiled."

Seneca waited for more but Allard's lips were sealed. Under the intense scrutiny, he knew he couldn't keep this secret to himself much longer. If Seneca asked directly, he would spill every sordid detail and hate himself for it.

"Was there anything else?"

Allard shook his head, lips pressed together.

For a moment, Seneca didn't move. Allard was sure that he was going to press the issue, but then, suddenly, he simply nodded and turned. He continued, leading Allard back to his room. At the door, he bid him goodnight but didn't say any more about the prisoner.

Once Allard was alone, he threw himself back against his bed, gaze flying to the ceiling.

Allard had kissed plenty of people before. He used to do it quite often. He liked flirting and sneaking away from an event to press his lips against some noblewoman's. Or even better, a peasant's. Someone his father would never approve of. It had always been exciting.

But then he'd realized that it wasn't supposed to end there and as he'd grown further into adulthood, more was expected.

He'd had sex once only, with Lady Leanina. She was beautiful and receptive and eagerly snuck away from the ball when Allard had suggested it. But she'd been unexpectedly forward and experienced, and Allard had simply followed her lead all the way through the act. It hadn't been bad. In a sense, it was good, the sensations enjoyable, but something about being pressed against her made him uncomfortable. At the time, he'd thought it was because he didn't know her well. Of course, lately, he knew that there was a different reason for his discomfort. He just wasn't attracted to women the way he should be.

He'd avoided that truth until witnessing Prince

Nemir and Soluc's love. Now, he knew it was true and that the type of love he wanted was possible, but didn't know what to do about it.

Fenian's kiss, the first he'd ever received from a male, went straight through his body most spectacularly.

How could he ignore that Fenian was supposed to be killed in the morning? How would he ever forget being someone's last desire?

CHAPTER 6

FENIAN

*F*enian's stomach was in knots, his cock rock hard, desperate for the human prince's lips once more.

He hadn't expected the prince—*Allard*—to be so immediately receptive to him.

When he'd first seen him, resentment had risen in him like bile. He was a spoiled, privileged, heir to a throne. He was everything Fenian hated. He stood above all, looking down at his people as though they were lower than him.

It had infuriated Fenian... but it had also given him an idea.

Not long ago, an oaf and a human prince bonded their lives together through marriage. Although it had been forced, the bond was harmonious and worked in the oaf's favor.

Fenian literally had a pile of bonding powder scattered across his floor.

When Seneca had insulted him, Fenian had reacted without thinking. He was strong, and more skilled in magic than any of the elders probably knew. Fenian could light a fire up to a mile away, and so, he *had*. For Fenian, setting the explosives storehouse alight had been easy.

The explosion drew Seneca and the guards away and all Fenian had to do was somehow reach the Prince's perfect golden locks.

He hadn't really thought it would work.

Trembling, Fenian looked down at his hand. In the dark of his cell, he could only see the shadowy shapes within, but he didn't need to see to confirm what he held, clutched in his palm like the lifeline that it was, was Prince Allard's *hair*.

It was the main component of the bonding spell. A bit of each of them, with the ancient incantation and a bit of fire, was all he needed.

His mouth went dry. Nerves and hope warred within him.

If he bound himself to Prince Allard, surely the human would stop his execution. He would feel compelled to protect his husband, even if he didn't know they were married. Then of course, if somehow they managed to *consummate* the relationship, their lives would be entwined. The elves wouldn't dare to carry out Fenian's execution or the human prince would die with him.

The plan was weak, but it was all he had, and yet, Fenian sat frozen in hesitation.

Yes, he would be alive, but he would be bound to someone for the remainder of his life. He would feel Allard's pain, know him more deeply than he knew another soul, he would become half of their union, rather than his own independent being.

Swallowing, Fenian thought of the prince.

His bright gray eyes were filled with uncertainty and naivety.

He was beautiful, Fenian had to admit. After all, he hadn't been *planning* to seduce Allard, he'd only wanted to reach his hair... but then he'd taken a long look at him, saw how sweet and full his lips were, *so inviting*, and felt the fear and desire in his gaze. He hadn't been able to resist.

But the one kiss wasn't enough.

His body was still rigid with want, breath still heavy. If he touched himself now, it would be to images of the prince on his knees with those soft lips wrapped around him.

Fenian shut his eyes and breathed deeply. Pleasuring himself would only seem unfair now when he knew that Allard would willingly lay with him if given the chance.

Fenian would never have him the way he wanted him… not unless he did this.

Decision made, he crouched to his knees and made a small light in the palm of his hand.

The pale blue glow illuminated the floor where he shined it. He had already used what he'd gathered of the healing powder and his body had recovered from the fall he'd suffered earlier in the day.

The red bonding powder was spread across the floor but some of the pile lay intact.

Carefully, he opened his other hand, dropping the short strands of hair on top of the pile, then reached up, combing fingers through his own hair, searching for loose strands. One came free and he gently laid it atop Prince Allard's. Blue on gold.

For a moment, he paused, second-guessing himself again until he realized; if the prince didn't try to stop the execution and Fenian died, there would be no repercussions to deal with. The spell would be broken. It was only if he survived that he would have to deal with being bound to Allard. He had to do this. It was his last chance at life.

Fenian shut his eyes, clearing his mind. For a moment, he had to search for the words, but then they came to him. The old elvish rhyme was danger-ously simple. Simple enough that even a child or an oaf could memorize it.

Still, he recited it carefully, enunciating each syllable and vowel in a careful whisper.

Then, he bowed his head and blew on the pile, gently enough that the hair and dust remained mostly undisturbed.

When he placed his hands over the dust to light it up, his heart stuttered a moment, but he ignored it.

The pile burst into flames, fire chasing the dust that had scattered across the floor.

Despite himself, Fenian took a shuddering breath as, just as suddenly, he was plunged into darkness once more.

For a moment, he sat back, completely still, wondering if the guards had seen the fire. No one came to his cell, so he supposed not.

Still, his body was trembling as he lifted a hand and shined a gentle light on where the dust had been. Only soot remained.

It was done.

Providing that he lived past the morning, he would not rest until he finished what he'd started with the human prince earlier.

Fenian would make love to him. He would utterly destroy any notion of pleasure that Allard had ever had before. He would make himself valuable. Irreplaceable.

He would live.

* * *

ALLARD

Allard awoke in a fevered sweat halfway through the night.

His prick was hard *again* and Fenian was in his thoughts. He tried to push them away but couldn't. His entire body was in turmoil.

Just as morning light touched his windows, a gentle tap on the door forced Allard to rise.

The cold tiles on his feet grounded him enough that he had the sense to pull his robe on. The thick fabric was much more efficient at covering the aroused state of his body than the thin cotton of his pajamas.

When he pulled open the door, Seneca was waiting patiently on the other side, hands clasped behind his back, expression grim.

"I apologize for disturbing you so early. May I come in?" he asked.

Allard moved aside, allowing the elf to enter his

small space. He shut the door behind him, fear gripping him.

"Did something happen?"

Seneca turned to face him.

"It is nearly time for the execution of our prisoner."

Allard's entire body went cold.

"Fenian."

Seneca nodded and all the air seemed to leave the room.

"His last request is for you."

For a moment, Allard only stared at him.

"What do you mean?"

"He has requested your presence at his execution."

For a moment, Allard's entire heart squeezed.

"But, *why?*"

Bitterness twisted Seneca's lips.

"Perhaps to taint you to the elves. He must know humans do not carry out executions. Fenian is conniving. With his last request, he means to destroy our developing alliance."

Allard shook his head. His hands were shaking.

"But—No. I can't—I *won't* watch an execution."

Seneca nodded. Even though his expression barely shifted, he seemed relieved.

"I expected as much. I will inform him."

He walked past Allard; the discussion done. Only as he opened the door did Allard suddenly stop him.

"Wait!" He swallowed and forced his voice out. "Was I really his last request?"

His voice was pathetically weak and small, and Seneca's gaze hardened.

"I already told you that," he reminded Allard. "Did you think I was lying?"

Swallowing, Allard shook his head.

"No. I'm sorry."

He took a deep breath, trying to calm nerves that had been frayed since last night.

"I'll come."

* * *

SENECA WAS silent as he led Allard, now dressed, to the place where executions were held.

To his surprise, it was an open field.

Along one side, there were benches to sit on. The others from the council were already seated. Behind them was a raised platform, on which five bowmen already stood in the green and gold uniforms that all the guards wore. Their bows were already drawn and ready.

When they entered, Seneca went to stand with them, and at a wave from Yana, Allard went to the benches, taking a seat with the council while nerves ate at him.

"It was kind of you to attend," Yana said.

Allard shook his head.

"I had no choice," he said, without thinking.

He could feel her eyes on him curiously but was too nervous to partake in any more chit-chat. Any minute now, Fenian would enter. Would they tie him to a seat? He assumed death would be delivered from the bowmen behind them. Were there so many so that no one knew whose shot delivered the killing blow?

Allard felt ill.

His leg was tapping, hands sweating.

Why had he agreed to this?

Probably because the poor soul had no one else to ask for. Why else would he request Allard's presence? Perhaps he didn't want to be alone, and he knew Allard now, in a way, even though their encounter had been brief. The thought sent an unbearable ache through his body.

Then, without any announcement or commotion, Fenian walked into the execution field, a guard on each side, holding his arms, which were cuffed behind his back.

Allard's breath hitched at the sight of him.

In the light of day, his hair gleaned, light brightening the blue in contrast to his pale skin and hard, angular features.

His gaze flickered to Allard as he walked, not brown as Allard had thought in the dark, but the same unearthly blue of his hair.

When their gazes mct, they didn't hold. Fenian immediately looked away, as though Allard wasn't even there, but there was a shift in him; a deep, subtle inhale as a small bit of tension left his shoulders. He was glad that Allard was here.

And Allard was devastated.

Fenian was taken to the center of the small field before them and then one of the guards stood back while the other removed his handcuffs.

Yana stood.

"Fenian," she said. "We hope that you choose to accept your death honorably and as the result of the damage you have caused. Do you have any last words?"

With a deep breath, Fenian turned his gaze to Allard.

"You can't let them do this," he said.

His voice rang clear in the quiet of the morning and the ever-present oppressiveness of the elves' homeland.

Shock ran through Allard.

"The human prince can do nothing to save you,"

Yana admonished, voice dripping with disappointment, but Fenian didn't so much as look at her. His desperate gaze remained on Allard, staring straight into his eyes.

Allard's hands were shaking, fear and literal pain squeezing him from the inside. Fenian was right. He couldn't let this happen.

"Let us not drag this on any longer," Seneca said from behind them. "Ready. Aim—"

Allard was on his feet.

He didn't remember moving, he hadn't planned on it, but before Seneca could utter the next word, he was dashing across the moss and grass.

Relief painted Fenian's expression, and he came forward, catching Allard just as Allard turned to face the others, heart in his throat, arms spread out to shield Fenian.

"You can't do this," Allard gasped.

His heart was racing so hard he could barely breathe. Fenian's arms went around him, hugging his midsection tightly. He pressed his face against the back of Allard's neck, using him as a shield, but it didn't matter because he was *against him.* They were so close. They were *together*. It was everything that Allard wanted. It was what he *needed.*

His feverish brain told him he'd lost it, as did the faces of the council members and the bowmen who had all lowered their arrows. Everyone watched Allard like he was completely insane.

He didn't care.

"Stay back!" he shouted when one of the guards took a small step toward them.

Everyone stilled except Seneca, who stepped from the platform and approached the field, tilting his head thoughtfully as he watched them.

"Prince Allard," he said gently. "Why are you doing this?"

Allard didn't know. He couldn't even begin to explain.

Fenian's embrace felt like every good thing in the world. If he died, there would be darkness and nothing else.

"I can't watch him die," he managed.

"Very well, then you can return to your room."

"No!" He swallowed, took a breath, and tried to explain. "I need... I need to be... with him..."

Confusion filled him.

Allard looked at the elven council, feeling lost as understanding crossed their faces.

"Fenian, what have you done to him?"

Suddenly, Allard was pulled backward. He stumbled into step as he realized what was happening. Fenian was pulling him away. He was going to run.

"Don't shoot or you'll kill him!" Fenian shouted.

Allard saw the conflicting emotions on the elves' faces.

"You won't make it far."

"Try to stop me," Fenian growled.

His voice, so near Allard's ear, sent a shiver straight through him.

Suddenly, they broke through the line of trees and Fenian released him, grabbing his hand and pulling.

"Come on!" he shouted.

The moment, Fenian released him, arrows whizzed past, narrowly missing them.

"You will never get away with using magic on the human prince!" someone shouted from behind them and then there was nothing but the sounds of their feet hitting the earth as they ran.

Fenian didn't look back at him, but he kept an iron grip on his wrist and Allard knew, he had no intention of letting him go. They were in this together.

CHAPTER 7

FENIAN

Fenian tore through the woods, Prince Allard's hand clutched in his own.

Fear and exhilaration and desire coursed through him, each battling to overtake the other.

It had been so close. One more minute and those arrows would have pierced his flesh. And he still wasn't free, not yet. They were semi-hidden for now. Using all the energy he had, he had created a force-field around them. No one would approach, but this wasn't Fenian's strongest skill set and he knew, it wouldn't last long.

"Stop," Allard gasped behind him, heels digging into the earth.

Panic seized him. Any minute now, they could be found. If they didn't do this now, it would all have been for nothing.

"Not yet, we're still too close. We must hide."

He yanked Allard forward, searching the trees for any bit of cover. The forest was dense, but the elves would track them quickly. They needed to hide properly.

Suddenly, Allard yanked Fenian to a stop, swinging him around so that they were facing each other, his handsome face twisted in fury.

"What did you do?" he demanded.

In response, anger grew within Fenian as well.

"I saved myself," Fenian spat. "What part of that is so hard to comprehend?"

Allard's jaw clenched and his hands fisted at his sides. He didn't stop there though. Without warning, he swung, narrowly missing punching Fenian across the jaw, only because he leaned just out of reach.

"I meant to *me*!" Allard shouted, swinging again. This time, Fenian caught his fist. "What did you do to me?!"

He threw the prince's fist down and stepped forward, right into his face, barely an inch between them.

"Nothing more than what you already wanted,"

he growled, and then, because being this close to Allard without touching him was agonizing, he grabbed him by the hips, gripping the fabric of his pants, and yanked him closer.

Their bodies met and he nearly cried with relief. Allard felt good. Better than anyone had any right to feel through so many layers of fabric. His gentle, clean smell and line of hard muscles nearly made Fenian's eyes roll with pleasure—and then he was shoved roughly away.

"You—you *made* me want you!" Allard accused.

Fenian grit his teeth.

He took another step toward the prince, glowering when Allard took a step back.

"You wanted me from the start," he said.

Allard began to shake his head which only infuriated Fenian more. He was *not* the only one who had been aroused last night when they'd met. Prince Allard had been an eager participant in that kiss.

Furious, he marched over to the prince, unsure what he was going to do.

Allard acted out as he neared, trying to push him back but Fenian caught him by the wrists, stopping him, and then suddenly, they were in a scuffle.

A knee struck Fenian's thigh, his fist met Allard's stomach. Together, they fell into the leaves and dirt,

Allard under him, and Fenian fought with all his might to keep him there as they struggled, each fighting for the upper hand.

Finally, Allard fell still, chest heaving.

He glared up at Fenian with those wide eyes that had been fixed on him in the fevered dreams he'd had all night.

"You honestly think you can convince me that you didn't want me?" Fenian asked quietly. "I was there. I could feel you... you were just as hard as I was."

Allard's entire face flushed red.

He took a deep breath as though to speak but seemed unable to find words. After a moment, he swallowed and tried, voice trembling.

"Then what were they talking about back there? They said you did something to me, and I felt—"

"Desire?" Fenian supplied.

Allard swallowed again and then nodded.

Even though he knew some of this was the effect of the bonding spell, pushing them to consummate the bond that had been started, the admission still made Fenian feel lighter than air.

He looked down at the human who was so incredibly cute and sexy at the same time. Initially, he had wanted to bond them together so that he could live, but at this moment, with the spell working its magic on them both, he was pleased to realize that being forced to make love to Prince Allard would be no hardship.

He'd thought as much already, but their brief, passionate kiss hadn't been enough to calm him over the permanence of his actions. This was it. They would be stuck together for the rest of their lives, and yet, that thought wasn't scaring him anymore. He was more interested in the long line of Allard's neck, the button that had ripped open and was exposing an inch of his chest. He wanted nothing more than to see what else lay beneath those cumbersome human clothes.

"I made you want me more desperately, is that such a problem?"

"What are you planning?" Allard asked, voice breathless and wary.

Fenian hadn't realized that he still needed to explain. He had thought the erection pressed against Allard's thigh was all the information that he needed to give, but perhaps humans needed things spelled out for them.

Heart racing, he released Allard's wrists, tracing his hands over his arms and shoulders until he reached his face.

Gently, he took it in his hands and leaned closer, so that only a hair's breadth separated them. He stared straight into Allard's eyes and pressed his hips down, feeling Allard's answering hardness against his leg.

"I don't want to hurt you," he breathed. "I want to make love to you."

For a moment, Allard stared at him, his body still. His mouth opened, but before he could say anything, their lips pressed together. Fenian didn't know who had moved first and he didn't care.

He groaned into the kiss, warmth, and happiness bubbling inside him, emotions as unfamiliar as they were pleasant. He didn't know what to do with the ecstatic feelings as they kissed, it was too much, so he bit into Allard's lips and ground down into him, perhaps too hard.

Allard gasped, tearing his lips away but his hands stayed on Fenian, holding him gratifyingly in place with a firm grip on his waist. He dove back up, pressing their lips together again, his hips tentatively moving against Fenian's.

It was too much and not enough all at once. And they didn't have much time. Panic rose in him but he swallowed it down. His forcefield would hold for now.

Still, he pulled back, bit the curve of Allard's jaw, then his neck. His heart squeezed at the sweet shiver that ran through Allard's body.

Fenian sat back trying to take his time to undo the copious buttons on the prince's shirt. It was ridiculous though and a garment as pompous as this didn't deserve to survive so he gripped the edges and tore it apart.

Allard gasped as his chest and abdomen were exposed and hunger, unlike anything that Fenian had ever felt filled him. These bonding spells were strong indeed because if he didn't bend down, and press his lips to the smooth expanse of Allard's warm-toned skin right now, he would probably die.

Moaning, Fenian dropped over him, lips licking his collar first, then dropping lower, gently kissing his chest before taking one soft pink nipple between his lips, relishing in the way it hardened against his tongue.

Allard's fingers suddenly laced into his hair. His soft moan pulled at Fenian's cock.

His whole body felt like it was out of his control. Never had he wanted someone like this. The desire was overwhelming; the bonding spell working its magic to ensure their partnership was consummated. The faster they did this, the sooner they would feel like themselves again so Fenian forced himself to move lower.

A soft trail of golden hair led down Allard's taut abdomen.

Unable to hold himself back any longer, he pulled the prince's pants down his hips, taking his undergarments with them and leaving the fabric tangled around his ankles.

Fenian breathed shakily, taking in the sight of the prince splayed open in front of him. His shirt was ripped apart, exposing his lovely chest and abdomen, his ankles were wrapped in fabric, his long, muscular legs stretched out, pink cock arched against his belly.

Fenian's mouth nearly watered at the sight of it, hard and glistening with need, nestled in the golden curls.

He was sure it hadn't been very long since he'd last had sex, but he could think of no one else. Allard was perfection. How lucky that the prince happened to be someone so in line with his tastes.

"Aren't you going to keep going?"

Allard's worried voice drew Fenian's gaze from his exposed body to the hesitant look clouding his eyes. Despite himself, Fenian felt the need to reassure him.

He crawled up Allard's body, aligning them long

enough to press a deep kiss to his lips. Allard responded almost desperately, tongues tangling, hands holding Fenian, pulling him down on top of him so that their hard cocks pressed together.

How had Fenian allowed his pants to remain on for so long, he wondered, annoyed by the constricting fabric.

Frustrated, he reached down, yanking his pants open, moaning in relief when their hard lengths pressed together.

For a moment, he could do nothing but bury his face into Allard's shoulder and thrust against him, pleasure overwhelming him, trembling already from his body's desperate desire for release. Of course, the way Allard clutched him, gasping, shaking, didn't help cool him off.

Taking a shuddering breath, he forced his hips to lift, groaning for a moment when Allard thrust up, following him with a desperate noise.

"We don't have much time," Fenian gasped. "I need to be inside you. Fast."

Prince Allard stilled.

"I haven't done this before," he said.

For a moment, Fenian's overheated brain couldn't quite comprehend what he meant.

"You're a virgin?" he asked incredulously.

To his relief, Allard shook his head.

"No, but I haven't ever—not with a man."

Fenian suddenly recalled something about this. Humans in Tasnia were forced to be heterosexual or something like that. It was rubbish of course, and he hadn't thought he would even run into any humans in his life, so he hadn't taken much stock of it before. Now though, he lifted his head to meet Allard's gaze, curious about what the prince was feeling. He hadn't shown any hesitance except when he thought Fenian had done something to him, which, he had, but that was beside the point. He had kissed him without needing the bonding spell. Perhaps he was getting a thrill out of doing something taboo.

There was nothing like that in his eyes though, just bare, open desire and uncertainty.

Shit.

Fenian couldn't enter him. He wanted to but for Allard's first time receiving, with no lubrication, laying in the dirt while Fenian *rushed* through their love-making session... He had been called a rogue before, but something inside him just wouldn't allow him to do it.

Regardless of what way they consummated, he wasn't going to last long. From the looks of it, neither would Allard.

He bent down, pressed a kiss to Allard's swollen

lips, and said, "Never mind, then. I will take you this time."

He kicked out of his pants and then straddled the prince once again. Allard's eyes widened as he watched Fenian reach behind himself without any ado.

Fenian's entire body was like a ring of tightly strung nerves. Even just touching himself with Allard's hungry gaze on him was nearly enough to undo him, especially when he pressed the tip of a finger inside.

He had to shut his eyes to cut out the image of the human prince. He'd never had anyone look at him in such a way and his heart was racing with unfamiliar shyness. *It's just the bond*, he reminded himself and a frisson of guilt filled him. Allard deserved to know the truth, but it was too late for that, and quite frankly, Fenian could not stop now. He wanted it too much, after all, the magic was affecting him too.

He pushed the thoughts away and tried to concentrate on what had to be done.

It took sucking on his fingers to wet them and then trying with all his might to clear his mind and relax his body to be able to take them.

It felt good enough, but it wasn't until Allard started touching him that he finally started to relax.

Allard's hands on his thighs, rubbing them, then tentatively touching his erection, stroking him up and down with light fingers had his tight hole clenching and loosening, desperate for more than a couple of fingers.

"Now," he gasped.

Fenian leaned forward, hand braced on Allard's chest and then gripped his lovely length, leading it to his loosened entrance.

Allard's tip was wider than Fenian's fingers and infinitely more welcome as he sat back onto it, groaning as he was impaled.

His head fell back, eyes squeezed shut as he was filled. For a moment it was too much, but he breathed through the discomfort.

Allard gasped under him, hands clutching him now, fingers digging into his thighs.

When Fenian started to move, they both cried out in pleasure. He fell forward, gripping the earth on each side of the prince as he rode him, twisting his hips so that pleasure sparked in him with every thrust.

"Fuck," Allard groaned. "I can't—"

He reached out desperately, hand seizing Fenian's cock, and with one hard, sloppy thrust into him, he came, stroking Fenian. The erratic movements of his tight fist combined with the feeling of his hot seed filling him were more than enough. Fenian's hole clenched, milking Allard's last few spurts as he spilled between them with a deep groan.

"Yes," Fenian sighed.

All the pent-up fear and anxiety left him, and he collapsed as the last of his orgasm ran through his body, leaving him pleased and sleepy.

"Thank you," he whispered. "It's done."

He started to laugh, a breathy, ridiculously happy noise that broke through the sounds of their combined heavy breathing.

He pulled himself off Allard, shivering at the loss of him inside, his body still prickling with pleasure, and rolled onto his side next to him.

"Thank you," he whispered, again. "We did it."

"Yes…"

Allard was watching him, a bemused smile on his face.

"We did do it," he agreed. "And it was probably the best thing that's ever happened to me."

Fenian laughed.

"Me too," he said, and then because he could hold in the truth no longer continued. "You've saved me. For real this time."

He swept in, kissing Allard again, overwhelmed with gratitude.

The prince wrapped his arms around him,

pulling him closer, and just like that, with their bodies entangling again, lips devouring one another's, both of their bodies began to react again.

"Mm," Fenian moaned, pulling back. He shook his head, gaze boring into his new husband's hungry eyes. He had to bite his lip to stop himself from kissing him again but that appeared to be too sexy an action for Allard to resist. His gaze dropped to Fenian's lips and he moaned, leaning in to lick them and making Fenian's head swirl.

"Stop," he groaned.

He pushed Allard back, putting proper space between them. For a moment, he couldn't remember why.

"My spell," he realized. He could already feel the edges of his magic waning, growing weaker. "It won't hold out much longer. We should probably get dressed before they find us."

Allard's face darkened. He sat up, looking down at Fenian, his expression grim.

"I promise you; I won't let them touch you," he vowed. "We should go. I'll take you home and—I don't know what exactly, but you won't be executed, not unless they want to deal with me."

"That is exactly what I planned for," Fenian informed him, rising.

His pants were lying discarded nearby, and he

went to them, pulling them on. He took a moment to ground himself before he turned to face Allard again.

The prince was sitting as he'd left him, mostly naked, hair disheveled, lips red and swollen, come drying on his chest.

They'd had a good time. Hopefully, that meant he wouldn't be too angry.

Just then, his forcefield faded, like a sigh releasing. His skin prickled, eyes darted around, seeking movement in the trees. They hadn't made it as far as he'd hoped, and they hadn't hidden at all. Any moment now, the other elves would be upon them.

"Get dressed," he ordered.

Startled, Allard reached down to his pants first. He had them wiggled halfway up his hips when suddenly, they were surrounded.

At least twenty of the elven guard stood in a circle surrounding them, arrows all pointing at Fenian.

Allard squeaked, yanking his pants up the rest of the way and scrambling in an attempt to button his destroyed shirt.

"Don't even think about firing at me," Fenian said calmly. "Unless you want the prince to die too."

"You fool! What have you done?" Yana demanded as the entirety of the council broke through the circle of guards and marched toward them, anger written across their faces but this time, Fenian wasn't at their mercy. Now, he was the powerful one.

A smile pulled at his lips.

"I did what I had to do."

CHAPTER 8

ALLARD

*A*llard couldn't follow the conversation. In part because he was absolutely mortified.

He scrambled to his feet, cheeks hot as he clasped his torn shirt across his midsection, hoping that the wetness seeping into the fabric from Fenian's release wasn't too obvious.

"Seize him," Seneca ordered and guards came forward gripping Fenian tightly by the arms—too tightly. Allard winced, for a moment, he was sure he was feeling the pain as though it was his own.

Fenian didn't react but his gaze flickered to Allard. The council members caught the look and their attention turned to him. Not one of them seemed to be disgusted by his behavior. On the contrary, they each watched him with profound sadness, which said a lot considering how much they hid their emotions.

"What is it?" Allard asked slowly.

Exchanging a look between them, Nellis, who seemed to be the gentlest of the five stepped forward.

"Fenian has bonded to you, Prince," she said. "We are truly sorry that we could not stop him before he caused this irreversible damage."

Still, Allard could not comprehend what was happening.

"Bonded?" he repeated.

"Once again," Kial said, his angry gaze fixed on Fenian. "You have destroyed someone's life for your own selfish needs."

"We hope you are happy," Elli added. Allard stared between them, his ears ringing.

Had Fenian destroyed his life? It hadn't felt like that. It had felt like every good thing in the world combined into one shared moment, their bodies entwined. Allard doubted that anything else would ever compare...and that was when it hit him.

Nemir. Soluc. They had been forced together through an elven bonding ceremony. It couldn't be. There had been no magic.

His eyes sought Fenian's. The elf was silent, gaze

fixed on Seneca's. They were silently talking, Allard realized. Probably shouting into each other's minds by the looks of it.

Then, with lips twisted in anger, Seneca motioned to the guards and they started to walk, pulling Fenian with them.

As they pulled him away, Fenian looked at Allard over his shoulder and *smiled* and the expression was so self-satisfied that Allard suddenly felt sick.

He'd dreamed of the elf all night. He would have done anything to be with him. Allard had barely been able to stop himself from throwing himself at Fenian, even after the others had pointed out that he had bewitched him.

A hand touched his arm, drawing him from his thoughts and he found that everyone had walked ahead. Yana remained, kindness in her pale eyes.

"I'm sure this is very shocking for you."

Allard managed to nod.

"It is a sacred bond that has been bastardized by that criminal, but we will help you."

Hope flickered inside him.

"You can cancel the bond?" he asked.

She shook her head.

"Not once it has been consummated. If we had known what he had done *before* you did, we could have annulled it. However, we can still reverse, or sever it."

He swallowed.

For some reason, his mother's words about Nemir's bond rang in his ears... it wasn't her problem because it wasn't her son...

He couldn't go home bonded to Fenian.

Allard nodded.

"Okay. We should sever it."

His heart felt like it was in a vice grip.

"Walk with me," Yana said.

Allard fell into step with her. Ahead, he could see the others. Flashes of midnight blue hair between the guards made his heart squeeze even harder.

"Everything I was feeling... it was all fake?"

"It was due to the bonding spell," she agreed. "When that spell is performed, it is not complete until the consummation and the spell *wants* to be complete. It makes individuals hunger for one another."

"So, he forced me to feel like that? Like I would die if we didn't... *consummate*?"

"He must have," she agreed. "Although I don't know how. Tell me, was there any moment you can think of before this morning when he could have taken some of your hair?"

Allard's stomach flipped.

Fenian had had his hand clenched in Allard's hair last night when he kissed him. At the time, Allard had thought it was only passion that made Fenian's grip so tight, yet he had been scheming the entire time.

"This can't be happening."

His whispered words came out without meaning to and for a moment, he had to stop, head bowed as he tried to breathe.

He'd never been so taken advantage of before. No one would have dared. Not even the oves. How ironic that they were the ones meant to be more barbaric, yet it was with the elves that Allard had been swindled.

"Tell me about the reversal," Allard forced.

"We on the council, each have roles," Yana said. "Seneca oversees the security and communication outside of the Elven Veil. Nellis monitors the balance within the community and Elli and Kial, enforce laws and punishments. As for me, I am the bonding and final hours overseer. Normally, I carry out the ceremonies. On very rare occasions, I reverse bonds. The spell is quite simple for me. You will feel almost nothing physically."

"*Almost* nothing?" Allard asked uneasily.

"Discontentment and emotional upheaval are the

main symptoms. In extreme cases, heart failure may occur."

Allard gulped.

"As I said, severance is extremely rare. It requires consent from both parties but in this case, I am willing to make an exception."

"Some heart cramps and depression," Allard said, shrugging, feigning indifference. "I can handle that. When can it be done?"

"The longer it is left, the deeper the bond will settle. We should do it today. At once. But prince, there is one more thing you must consider."

She came to a stop, waiting for him to do the same and fixing those unearthly pale eyes on him.

"Once a bond has been removed, a new one can never be made."

Allard shook his head, at a loss.

"I never intended to bond to an elf or oaf or anything," he reassured. "Humans don't do spells for a marriage."

She smiled sympathetically.

"Yes, I know, but it does not only apply to magic bonds. You will never feel love or passion the way that you can now with Fenian. Or even the way that you felt it before."

Allard stared at her.

"I don't understand. I won't love or feel desire again?"

"You will, I'm sure, but a duller version of it. You see, the bond fuses to your very being, reversing it effectively takes something from you with it."

Allard shook his head.

The way he'd wanted Fenian, the way his stupid body felt even now at the thought of him was *everything*.

Was it really worth undoing it?

"I've never felt like this before," he said.

"But do you want to feel this way with someone like Fenian?"

Allard honestly didn't know.

Despite himself and even though Fenian hadn't asked politely first, he couldn't pretend that he hadn't wanted to sleep with him from the start. The rogue elf had fulfilled all of Allard's desires while saving himself from execution.

Allard had wanted a way out of the future his parents wanted for him. Fenian had given him that and it came with his incredible body, ethereal appearance, and criminal ways.

Allard didn't know what to do.

CHAPTER 9

FENIAN

*D*espite the hands holding his arms as he was led through the trees back toward the city, Fenian felt like he was walking on air.

His body felt good, relaxed, and satisfied.

Somewhere behind them, his bonded husband was following.

He hadn't originally done it to win the prince over, but what a bonus it was.

Fenian looked over his shoulder, seeking the prince out, and was disappointed to find he couldn't see him.

They made it back onto the paths and then onto the outskirts of the Elven Veil. He recognized the direction they took back to the cells and a bitter laugh left him.

"Shouldn't you be taking me to the prince's room?" he asked loudly. "Surely, putting his husband into a cell is frowned upon."

One of the barred doors was opened and Fenian was shoved roughly inside.

As it was pulled shut and locked, Seneca stood watching him, coldness in his eyes.

"I never imagined you would take such cruel, selfish actions today."

"No, you thought I would die like a good little dawna."

"I will be the one to speak to the human king," Seneca went on. "You will pay for what you have done."

"Only if you want poor, innocent Prince Allard to suffer along with me," Fenian spat.

His stomach twisted with guilt at the description. Allard really *was* innocent in this.

"You're more foolish than I thought if you truly believe the bond will be left intact."

With that, Seneca shook his head, giving him one last, disappointed look before departing, leaving Fenian staring after him, his heart racing in shock.

He hadn't thought of that. No one had their bond reversed. It could be done, and sometimes was but only to save someone from their partner's imminent death. Those occasions were extremely rare. He hadn't even considered that it would be done now. It made sense though. If they reversed the bond and Allard was free from him, they could carry on with his execution.

Fenian stood there, stunned as he realized that all of his efforts were for nothing.

Then he remembered Allard under him, the expression of pure wonder and ecstasy on his face. *Maybe not* nothing *then...*

* * *

OVER THE HOURS Fenian sat alone in his cell, watching the breeze blow the leaves in the trees beyond, he came to some sort of peace over the whole situation. It was Allard's doing. The human wasn't even with him, but just knowing that he wasn't alone in this, somehow eased his restless spirit.

They didn't know each other well, but he would bet that Prince Allard was as kind as Fenian was ruthless. It made him feel strange being tied to someone like that. Their spirits were literally entwined now. Maybe that was why he felt such uncharacteristic disappointment in himself.

He hadn't let his thoughts linger too long on his crimes since he'd committed them and there were quite a few to be forgotten. Some he'd been caught for, others he hadn't.

He'd started young. Mostly stealing as a child, although occasionally, when he'd realized his strength with fires, he'd enjoyed destroying places too. He wondered what Prince Allard would think of that. He wondered what he would think of Fenian's most recent crime, his reason for being next in line for execution. Somehow, he knew the prince wasn't informed of them, otherwise, he never would have allowed Fenian to touch him.

When the guards returned for him, Fenian was not surprised.

Now that he and the prince were married, he would have to be dealt with as soon as possible.

Handcuffs were clasped around his wrists, biting into the bone in a way that was now familiar to him but to his shock, when he was taken from his cell, he was not led to the execution field, or even to the council, instead, he was taken back into the woods.

"Where are we going?" he asked, but no one answered him.

Eventually, they emerged onto one of the main paths—one that was used by all for shipments and travel.

There, waiting for them, was an ornate carriage and Prince Allard.

The relief he felt at seeing him was overwhelming. It was like he'd been holding his breath all this time and hadn't known.

"Allard," he said, stepping toward him, but the prince took a step back. He took a breath, gaze fixed on the well-beaten path.

"Take his handcuffs off," he ordered.

"But prince."

"*Now.*"

Fenian smiled at the imperious tone. He liked that Allard could be bossy, even if he was currently ignoring Fenian.

That wouldn't do.

He managed to remain silent as the door was held open for him and he stepped inside, taking a seat.

Prince Allard followed, taking the spot across from him.

"Where to?" he asked the moment he was seated. "Please tell me we are going on our honeymoon?"

Allard blushed that lovely deep peach color but didn't answer or look at him. Instead, he turned his attention out the window at the elven guard on horses surrounding them and nodded.

The carriage started to move and Fenian sat

back, eying his husband with a calculating gaze. Wherever they were going, it wasn't to get the bond reversed, at least there was that.

And Allard was cute when he was upset. The way his lips pouted made Fenian want to cross to his side of the carriage and kiss them gently, to taste his anger and turn it into something far more fun.

For a while, they rode in silence. Fenian waited stubbornly for Allard to speak until finally, he could take it no longer.

He kicked Allard's boot to draw his gaze.

"Come on, it's not so bad," he said, offering a smile, but Allard's expression only darkened further.

"Perhaps for you. You get to live a while longer, while I get to live with *you*. Knowing that I allowed you to do this to me."

"We enjoyed each other," Fenian reminded him.

"That was your doing," Allard said, jaw set in anger. "Your spell made me do it."

Fenian laughed at that.

"Don't lie to yourself prince," he snapped. "Or are you forgetting that the only reason I was able to get close enough to you, to begin with, was because you approached me while I was imprisoned? You wanted me from the start."

Allard turned to look out the window, jaw set.

For a minute, silence rang between them until Allard finally broke it.

"You robbed me of any future happiness I might have had. Either I'm stuck *with* you or stuck *remembering* you. Those are my only options."

Fenian swallowed.

For once, he had nothing to say. How was he supposed to defend his actions? How, when he couldn't even find it in himself to regret them? If there was anyone he could have been bonded to, Prince Allard was the one he would have wanted. He had lucked out in all ways.

"There must be *something* good about being bound to me," he muttered.

"Perhaps if you had told me that you were doing it and I'd agreed, I'd be able to think of something... as it stands, I'm devastated."

Fenian swallowed the bitterness rising in him, but he couldn't help some of it leaking out in angry words.

"Have you ever thought that I was doing you a favor?"

"A favor?" Allard demanded.

"Yes. A favor. Because you're so pent up, anyone could see a mile away how badly you needed to be fucked."

Allard stared at him, incredulously.

"I believe *I* was the one who fucked *you*," he reminded him.

"See?" Fenian snapped. "As I said, I was doing you a favor."

"Selflessly offering yourself to me for life, how very kind of you," Allard said dryly. "Believe it or not, I didn't need help finding someone to sleep with. I happen to be very attractive."

"And so humble too."

"Why is it that you were to be executed?" Allard suddenly demanded, changing the direction of the argument. "I foolishly thought that the elves were too strict. That you couldn't have done anything bad enough to warrant death. Now I'm not so sure."

Silence fell between them. Fenian's jaw clenched this time.

Why was it that he was so bothered by Prince Allard's judgment? His foot tapped anxiously. His heart pounded. He couldn't let it go.

"What I did," he suddenly said, unable to hold it in any longer. "I didn't deserve to die for… I performed the bond because…"

He searched for an explanation that didn't sound as selfish as it was, but couldn't find anything, so he settled on the truth.

"I'll admit, I hesitated at first, but you seemed to

feel something for me and I for you... and I was *desperate*."

Allard was watching him closely, the anger in his eyes shifted to something else, something that was hard to read, and then the wheels started clattering over uneven cobblestones. Fenian looked out the window, surprised to see that they were already going through a human city.

Small houses and buildings were erected, completely in the open. There were no trees whatsoever, only the bright open sky stretched above. People were everywhere, humans laughing and talking and shouting. It was a thousand times louder than the Elven Veil and full of that much more *life*.

Fenian couldn't stop staring in wonder. Around him, humans stared back, in awe of all the elves riding through the city and perhaps also of the prince visible in the ornate carriage with him.

Humans were all such lovely shades of browns and peaches, earthly, like the animals of the forest.

Then, when he saw the castle in the distance growing larger, a big imposing stone figure against a gray sky, he finally realized that Allard had been taking him home this whole time.

Hope swelled in him, and his gaze sought the prince's.

Allard was watching him. Sadness was now written across his face.

"What is it?"

"This isn't going to be pretty," Allard warned.

Frowning, Fenian looked back out the window as they drew up to the castle and his heart fell.

There, waiting for them, were countless knights and two people standing in the front, wearing tall crowns, fury written across their faces. Seneca stood next to them.

Fenian could only assume that the human king and queen were not very happy to have missed the wedding.

CHAPTER 10

ALLARD

"I suppose it's too much to assume that I'll be staying with you in the palace?" Fenian asked, lips twisted as the carriage drew to a stop.

Prince Allard's stomach clenched with nerves. He didn't bother answering. He didn't know what was going to happen, only that he'd refused to have the bond reversed and that meant delivering the news to his parents. Seneca had departed immediately while Allard gathered his belongings and his bearings. By now, they would already know.

The door swung open for them, and Allard stepped out, his heart racing as he saw his parents. His mother looked like she'd swallowed a lemon and his father was red with fury. Neither of them looked at him though, their gazes were fixed behind him at Fenian who was just emerging from the carriage.

As his feet touched the ground, the king marched toward him, lips pulled back in a snarl.

Allard didn't know what his father was going to do. He wasn't a violent man though so when he swung at Fenian with a hard right hook, Allard was completely caught off guard.

Pain burst across his jaw, sending him stumbling back as though *he'd* been hit.

The carriage caught him just as his father gripped Fenian by the collar of his shirt, yanking him forward roughly. Allard could feel the bruising force with which the fabric tightened around Fenian's neck, just like he had with the handcuffs.

"What have you done to my son?" the king demanded, spittle flying.

"Jareth!" His mother's voice rang through the air frantically as she tore after her husband, followed by Seneca.

"Your highness, stop."

"Let him go," his mother shouted, pulling his hands away from Fenian's neck.

He shook her off until she pointed at Allard.

"Look at him!"

King Jareth finally glanced at his son. He froze

for a moment, eyes fixed on the way Allard was leaning back on the carriage, hand still covering his father's phantom strike.

"I didn't know you could hit so hard," he said, feigning indifference.

Slowly, the fury on his father's face morphed into blank control.

He released Fenian and stood straight.

The king was tall and broad and as such an imposing figure, it somehow made Fenian look powerless compared to his inimitable father.

"Take him to the dungeons," he said and with that, turned on his heel and marched back toward the castle steps.

He didn't say anything to Allard, but he knew when he was to follow.

His mother gave him a look, eyes filled with fear and tears then she reached out, quickly squeezed his hand in her own, and went after her husband.

Seneca nodded to Allard grimly before going after her.

Standing exactly where he had landed, Allard still didn't feel like he could lift himself. He didn't feel like he could walk into his home alone. He needed someone to push him. He didn't want to face what his father had to say. He didn't want to talk about what had happened.

Even though he knew Seneca had already informed them of his bond and what that entailed, he wanted to pretend nothing had changed. But with Fenian here with him, how was he supposed to do that?

"Are you really going to let this happen?"

Fenian's sharp voice drew his gaze.

He was held by two guards, being physically forced in the direction of the dungeon entrance, but he was watching Allard, his gaze fixed on him over his shoulder. Frustration and anger in his eyes and Allard nearly snapped.

Shaking, he pushed himself up, standing tall.

"It's the least I can do," he said and waved farewell, at least for now, to his current husband.

His hands were still shaking when he marched into the castle. He felt ill and like he couldn't breathe, but he tried not to let it show as he hurried up the steps into the entrance hall.

It was empty save for Sten. The older man was standing by the door waiting for him with a warm towel, a glass of water, and a grim look.

He handed him the towel first and Allard took it, rubbing it gratefully over his face before handing it back.

Sten took it and handed him the water before leading him inside.

"They're in the second conference hall," he said, "waiting for you."

Allard nodded, bracing himself as he walked.

"Did you hear what happened?" he asked.

"Yes, sire."

Allard glanced at his manservant, wondering what he thought of the whole ordeal.

"Does it disgust you?" he couldn't help asking just as they reached the door.

Sten stopped and turned to face him, making sure Allard met his gaze.

"Not in the least," he said and Allard knew he meant it.

Somehow, that gave Allard the strength to take a deep breath and enter the room with his head held high.

Around the large, rectangular table, Allard, Seneca, his mother, father, and advisors were seated in silence, clearly waiting for him.

Swallowing, Allard went to the seat next to his mother and sat.

The moment he did, his father spoke.

"Explain how this happened."

It took Allard a moment to accept the fact that his father most likely wanted his full side of the story. Well, that wasn't going to happen. He would skim the details like his life depended on it.

"Seneca was giving me a tour," he began. "I wanted to see the prison so that was the first place we went—"

"Why would you want to go there of all places?" King Jareth interrupted. "Of all the foolish—"

"Let him continue," his mother said, stopping what was sure to be a tirade.

The king pursed his lips and waited.

"The prison had been mentioned over dinner, and I was interested," Allard explained, "but when we went there, there was an explosion. Seneca ran to deal with it, which was when Fenian took some of my hair for the spell. The next day—"

"How *did* he get so close?" Seneca interrupted this time. "He *was* behind bars."

Allard felt his cheeks heat as he met the green-haired elf's curious gaze.

"I—well, you see, I backed toward the bars at the explosion," he finally said.

"And he plucked out your hair and you thought nothing of it?" his father demanded.

Allard shook his head, flustered.

"No. Well, I didn't know he did. He just—he started talking to me and—and poking me and—I just thought he was trying to annoy me."

The lie was very unconvincing, even to his own ears.

A long silence fell over the room and Allard couldn't take it. Just as he was about to give in and spout every last detail of their heated kiss, his father sighed heavily and turned his attention to Seneca.

"It can't be that simple," he said. "It must take more than someone's hair to marry someone, otherwise there would be pure chaos in the Elven Veil, would there not?"

Seneca nodded.

"You are correct. It requires a strong spell caster a specific incantation and also, a certain powdered element that has been made by a master magic craftsman. Usually, the ceremony is performed by a strong elf. We hadn't realized that Fenian was on that level."

Allard was frowning now.

"Surely he didn't have access to the powder while he was imprisoned."

Seneca pursed his lips and shook his head.

"There was an incident," he confessed. "Earlier in the day, Fenian attempted to escape before falling into the storehouse and landing in the powders. At the time, it didn't seem feasible that he could collect any of it from his clothing, but that is what we now assume he did."

A laugh burst from his father's chest, drawing all the eyes in the room.

"Either that elf in our dungeon is the luckiest bastard that ever lived, or he is the most conniving."

"You really think he planned all that?" his mother asked thoughtfully.

"He couldn't have," Allard said, frowning. "I went to the Elven Veil on a whim. How would he have known I would be there?"

His mind was reeling, a strange feeling settling over him. Fenian's words in the carriage rang in his ears.

"Perhaps everything fell into place for him. Perhaps it was meant to be…"

Silence fell over the room, so thick, Allard's sharpest sword would have trouble penetrating it.

He looked at his father, the anger that had settled over his face was unmistakable.

"You claim that there is no way to kill the elf without harming my own son," King Jareth suddenly said to Seneca, as though Allard hadn't spoken.

Seneca shook his head.

"They are physically bound as well as spiritually. Any harm that befalls Fenian will be directly felt by Prince Allard. If Fenian dies now, your son will go with him."

His mother sniffled.

"What should we do?" King Jareth asked, finally turning to his two advisors for support.

"Reverse the bond," one of them said. "It will be unpleasant, but better than having the heir to the throne bound to a criminal who is not human *or* female."

"No," Allard said at once. "I won't allow that. It's *my* life that will be affected, my ability to love again. You told them that, didn't you?"

Seneca nodded.

"Better yet, leave the bond intact," the other advisor cut in, making Allard's heart soar for a moment before he went on. "Keep the elf in the dungeon to rot but keep him alive and comfortable enough that it will not impact Prince Allard's life. His fate was doomed anyway, and an elven bond will not stop Allard from marrying another."

Allard's chair clattered behind him as he suddenly rose, breathing hard, confused as to why he wanted to suddenly defend Fenian to such a degree.

"You can't do that."

"And why not?" his father asked, thoughtfully. "It seems like a viable answer to our issue. It is an unfortunate position that you find yourself in, but forget about him and carry on."

Allard shook his head, frantically.

"It's cruel," he said.

"I have to agree," Seneca added, and his father's face went red with anger.

"Is it crueler than the execution he was to be dealt with?"

"An execution is quick," Seneca said. "And it was our choice to make. After all, he is an elf. In the end, it is our choice how he should be punished."

"Even when it impacts my son?" the king demanded.

"Stop!"

Allard's voice ringing into the room halted the forming argument.

"Fenian is *mine*. It should be my choice what happens to him."

Even Allard was shocked by the words that came out of his mouth.

He hadn't meant to say them. They'd just come out without thinking and now, everyone was watching him with wide eyes… except for Seneca, who didn't seem very surprised by this at all.

Slowly, his father pushed to his feet.

"You are not in your right mind," he said. "Go to your room and don't worry about any of this. It will be dealt with."

He nodded to the doorman who immediately held the door open for Allard.

Stunned, Allard didn't know what to do but follow his father's orders.

As soon as he stepped into the corridor, the door was sealed shut behind him.

For a moment, he stood there, unsure what had happened, then, he heard Seneca's muted voice carried through the thick wood.

"You are right. Fenian must be punished."

"Prince Allard," Sten's gentle voice drew his attention.

Allard hadn't even noticed him waiting there for him.

"Come, I have dinner waiting for you."

Allard managed a nod and followed his manservant back to his room. The moment he entered the familiar chamber, he asked for privacy and sealed the door shut behind him.

He felt strangely numb.

So much had happened in such a short time, Allard didn't know how to process it.

He'd had his first kiss with a male and he'd loved it. He'd been so attracted to Fenian from the start that when they'd run into the woods together, fallen to the ground, and passionately made love, it had felt more natural than anything. It hadn't felt forced. It hadn't felt like insidious magic, and Allard supposed that was because it wasn't. That spell was meant to be used for marriage, after all. It was for two consenting individuals to form a deeper bond and understanding of one another. It was meant to add love and companionship to one's life.

Was Fenian now Allard's only hope for that? Was that why he so rebelled against his father's plans for the elf?

CHAPTER 11

SENECA

The door to the meeting room sealed shut with a soft click. All the humans watched each other with fleeting, somber glances.

"You are right. Fenian must be punished," Seneca said, breaking the silence. "But I must insist that his punishment be directly decided by the elven council. As the elven representative, I must inform you that we will not take kindly to you taking the decision into your own hands for one of our own."

How King Jareth managed to govern an entire country of humans was a mystery to Seneca. He was so unable to dilute his frustrations that he constantly seemed to be on the verge of bursting. Case in point, his lips pursed at Seneca's words, and his face turned a deep, angry red.

It couldn't be good for his heart.

"My son is the one who now suffers, at the hands of your *elven council*," he grit out. "As far as I am concerned, this is an attack on my family and the human kingdom itself!"

Spittle flew from his lips, spraying the table and even Seneca's hand which rested atop the smooth wood.

His lip curled in distaste despite himself. He took the time as the advisors began to whisper placating sentiments to the king to carefully wipe his hand clean with a handkerchief from his pocket.

"Let us discuss this calmly," one of the advisors was saying. "We do not want to start a war, King Jareth."

"No, please," the Queen jumped in. "We were meaning to make connections with the elves, not to create a new enemy within our land."

She looked at Seneca, offering him an apologetic smile. Finally, the King seemed to deflate, but only slightly. His gaze, when he fixed it on Seneca was still guarded and cold.

"King Jareth," Seneca began, "your son was the target of an outlaw who was already forsaken by the elves. In this situation, we have all been played by Fenian's hand."

The king's jaw grit and he nodded.

"You are right. And he deserves the punishment you had arranged for him. Sever their bond. Carry on with his execution. Free my son."

Seneca managed not to shift in his seat as his conscience immediately made itself known.

He could not sever a marriage bond without the consent of the couple. It was wrong on such a deep level that he would never forget it and never forgive himself.

"Your son does not want the bond severed. He has already formed an attachment to Fenian. His soul—"

"He will move on."

"I'm afraid that's not true. For the remainder of his life, he will feel lost without his bonded husband."

The queen visibly paled, the king's gaze fell to the table.

For a moment, Seneca was hopeful and then he realized what he truly wanted; a small punishment for Fenian and then the time and chance for his redemption.

Despite his position, Seneca had always been far too sensitive. A large part of him had been against the execution from the start. Knowing what he knew about Fenian's life, his upbringing, and his final crime... it sat within him like a ball of lead. It made him feel slightly ill, but he trusted his comrades, and being as diplomatic as he was, he went with the majority vote.

Now he realized just how much his decision came with the sacrifice of his own morals.

"Sever the bond or start a war with the humans. The choice is yours."

For a moment, King Jareth's words hung in the air. Queen Barnett sniffled but there was no other sound or movement as they all waited for Seneca's response.

"I will not be bullied into an immediate decision," he said calmly. "I will return to the Elven Veil and discuss our options with the council."

"What options?" King Jareth demanded.

"Whether we conform to your threats," Seneca snapped, "or prepare for battle."

He didn't often lose his cool, but the humans seemed devoid of the ability to control their tongues, more willing to start a fight than find a resolution.

"Make no mistake," he said, pushing to his feet. "You're threatening a nation that is more than well equipped to destroy your blundering human army."

The king rose to his feet, looking down his nose at Seneca.

"So that is your decision?"

"No. Unlike you, I will not allow my temper to dictate me. I will go to the elven veil and meet with the council, as I stated. Do not forget that it is one of *our* people you have in your dungeon and that I delivered him in hopes we would work through this amicably. If there is a war it will be of your making."

A long silence stretched at Seneca's words until finally, the king spoke.

"When will you return with your decision?"

"We will need time to deliberate," Seneca said, relieved that the argument was over at least for now. "I will send word as soon as possible."

The king nodded and that was the end of the tense discussion. Seneca could not wait to remove himself from the human kingdom and return home.

There was something about being here, away from nature, that set him on edge. More than that though, he wanted time to *think*.

It would only take a few hours to return to the Elven Veil and it wasn't enough time to process the extent of his churning thoughts.

Fenian, once a small child under Seneca's guidance was now in a cell in the human kingdom. Pure desperation to live had pushed him to this point and, if Seneca was being honest, he was glad.

Genuine relief filled him that the wayward elf had been so reckless that he had found a way to escape his execution.

Although he had thrown the entire elven community into hot waters with the humans, it had been a brilliant plan in a way.

After all, now the prince himself fought to keep him alive.

Then again, at the cost of a war with the humans, it still might not be enough.

Frustrated, Seneca was forced to face one hard fact. He had disrespected his own beliefs out of respect for the council. *That* was a grave injustice to himself. If he had insisted on a different punishment for Fenian, they wouldn't be in this situation, to begin with.

He wasn't foolish enough to blame himself entirely. Oh no, Fenian needed to change too.

Perhaps finding love would do the trick.

FENIAN

FENIAN STOOD IN HIS CELL—IF one could call it that. It was more like a cave with bars on it.

He'd nearly died of shock when he'd been pushed into the dark tunnels below the castle.

By torchlight, he had seen the uneven earth and stone of the tunnels as they'd walked and at times, crawled through. When they reached his cell and pushed him inside, genuine panic had risen in him. It was nothing more than a small space that had been cleared of earth. He could stand straight only in the front, near the bars, the rest was curved and sloped surfaces.

It was muddy, windowless, damp, and cold.

There was nowhere to sit or sleep.

To top it all off, when the guards had left, they'd taken all but one torch with them.

Now, Fenian stood in despair, watching the flame. It was growing dim already. Soon he would be in utter darkness.

Were they really going to leave him down here indefinitely? Would Prince Allard allow it?

The flames flickered, throwing deep shadows on all of the jagged stone.

Fenian held his breath, staring at the flame. It didn't go out, just settled back to the steady, flickering and he sighed in relief.

He really had taken his cell in the Elven Veil for granted, hadn't he?

How ironic that in escaping it, he had simply traded in his cell for an even worse one. In his old cell, he could see the sky. He was outdoors, watching the days pass, the animals in the trees beyond. He had fresh air and a bed. It was practically luxurious compared to this.

Again the torch fire flickered.

Fenian looked at it, willing the thing to stay lit, just as it went out, plunging him into darkness.

Heart hammering his ribs, he reached out blindly until he found the bars.

For a moment, he held onto the cold metal, attempting to calm himself down. Then, he held out his hand and produced a small, glowing blue light.

He was strong in his magic. He could give himself light for a while, but it would drain him slowly and steadily. He couldn't keep it on constantly.

Taking a deep breath, Fenian wondered what to do.

As he stood there, Allard and his human family were probably trying to decide exactly that. But what options would they have except to remove Fenian from this pit eventually and accept him as a new member of their family?

Surely, they didn't intend to just leave him down here.

A hysterical bubbling rose in his chest and burst from his lips in a laugh that echoed eerily off the uneven walls.

If they kept him down here, alive but out of the way... that would be the ultimate solution to their problem, wouldn't it?

His hands gripped the bars now, so tightly that his knuckles were white.

As the hours passed, Fenian found a spot on the floor to sit while his mind wandered. There was nothing else he could do but think.

He already felt like he was losing his mind. He could not remain down here. He wouldn't survive. Nor would Allard.

Allard.

His name was oddly soothing, even just to think. Like before, knowing that they were connected, that he wasn't completely alone, comforted him.

What he wouldn't give to see him, to talk to him... if only Allard could use inner speak, the way the elves could, then they could converse even now. Perhaps then Fenian could convince him to release him...

Slowly, he sat straighter, curiosity sparking in him.

They were bound now on such a deep level that their souls were connected. Perhaps they *could* speak. They were close enough, he was sure. After all, they were in the same building, Allard above, Fenian below…

He shut his eyes, searching for Allard's presence within him. With other elves, it was easy. He just spoke as though they were there and could hear him and up to a certain distance, it always worked. He would just have to do it the same way with Allard.

Prince Allard, can you hear me?

Fenian waited.

There was no reply.

Not even a breath or sigh or stirring came from his husband.

He swallowed and tried again. Perhaps Allard couldn't answer.

If you can hear me, imagine my face and speak your reply silently to me. I will hear you.

That was how the technique was originally taught to children. First, they practiced while looking at one another, then with their eyes closed, then with more and more distance between them. Hopefully, Allard was a quick learner.

Again, there was no reply.

For a while, Fenian fooled himself into thinking the prince was busy. Perhaps he was with others and couldn't reply. Better yet, he was probably alone in his bedroom, eyes squeezed shut, wishing desperately to talk to Fenian, trying to be heard with all his might.

By the time Fenian's light and energy began to dwindle, he accepted the truth. *If* Prince Allard could hear him, he probably had no interest in talking.

He couldn't help remembering the way they'd argued in the carriage, the bitterness in his voice. Not to mention the fact that Allard's family hated Fenian for what he had done.

He reached up in the dark, gingerly touching the bruise on his jaw.

Of course, it made sense for Allard to choose his family over Fenian, but for some reason, it was hard to stomach. He wanted to be more important, as irrational as that was.

I can't believe you would leave me here, he said to prince Allard. *Not that I was expecting a warm reception, but a dungeon is rather extreme.*

Again, there was no answer.

The lights have gone out. Both the torch and my magic... It is very quiet down here. I may as well have already been buried. Perhaps I have. Did I die as scheduled at my execution, Prince? Is this some form of torture only known in the afterlife?

He laughed at the thought.

Come to think of it, everything from this day has felt like a dream... but not all of it was torturous. Having you in the forest was more like bliss, so this must be real, after all.

He didn't know why he kept talking. Probably on the off chance that the prince would suddenly start to hear him. No, that wasn't true. The only reason Fenian tried to speak to Allard now was that he knew he *couldn't* hear him.

It was strangely freeing to know that he could say absolutely anything and receive no judgment in return.

His head fell back against the rough stone, and he shivered.

It's cold down here, he whispered. *What I wouldn't give to be wrapped around you, as we sleep tonight... Ridiculous, I know. I should be used to being alone by now.*

The truth of that statement hit Fenian like a punch to the gut. With a shuddering breath, he accepted images from over the years, of his parents, friends and teachers, the council, a horde of people who had let him down.

And he was to blame.

Even with a soul bond, nothing has changed. I never deserved love. I still don't.

CHAPTER 12

ALLARD

*A*llard lay in his bed, hands clutching the blankets, eyes fixed to the ceiling, a lump clogging his throat.

I was made to feel alone. To die alone. I should have known that dragging someone else into my life would only add to the long list I should probably repent for.

Fenian's voice whispered softly in Allard's mind, making him shiver.

Why could he now hear him so clearly? All evening, Allard had heard Fenian's voice like he was calling him from another room. He'd been muffled and unclear.

He'd realized what it was at once. The elves had told him about inner speak. It hadn't occurred to him that bonding with an elf would allow him to use it. It seemed to be one-sided though, something for which, Allard was glad, because if he could answer Fenian, what would he say? Would he even *want* to interrupt?

Never had someone whispered their innermost, intimate thoughts to him before. It was like being under a spell that Allard didn't want to break, even though he knew it was wrong to listen. He didn't want Fenian to stop.

The way he spoke about Allard in the forest had made his heart ache, but the way he spoke about *himself* now, made it ache even more.

Alone. Always alone. Since I was a child. Did you know that? Everyone in the Elven Veil knows. They all watched me grow, offering nothing but distance. Then, of course, they all grew to hate me.

Allard swallowed. A small stirring of guilt filled him.

Fenian didn't want him to hear all of this. He didn't want him to know. Yet, Allard didn't move. He remained so still, heart hammering his ribs as he laid there, as though his movement would disturb the flow of Fenian's confessions.

What had happened to him? Allard wondered. Alone as a child... he couldn't imagine it. And although his stay in the Elven Veil had been short and he hadn't seen as much of it as he had been hoping to, he hadn't seen anything like street people there. Would a child truly be left alone? Surely someone would care for them. Where had Fenian's parents been?

For a long time, there was silence and Allard assumed that Fenian was done sharing. Maybe he'd fallen asleep.

Allard hoped so. At least one of them should rest and he was wide awake.

He wished Fenian would continue to talk about him. His ego craved more adoration, and he didn't even know what to make of *that*. He'd always wanted it from people. He went out of his way for it, dressing well, charming anyone he met.

Allard loved the smitten looks people gave him. Strangely, it fulfilled him. He wanted to be important. As though being the prince of Tasnia wasn't enough. How ungrateful was he?

From a distance, Allard could see that he was trying to fill something within him. Something that for a few minutes, in Fenian's arms, he'd felt for real.

Why was it that the first person to make Allard feel something so deeply was only using him? He couldn't even pretend it was the bonding spell because the moment he'd seen Fenian step out from the shadows in his cell, his heart and body had reacted.

Somehow, lost in his thoughts, Allard began to doze.

Is it morning yet? Allard awoke to Fenian's quiet voice in his mind. It was so unusual, so intimate but felt as natural as his own thoughts. *It's so dark down here.*

Allard's eyes fluttered open.

It was indeed morning. Soft light flooded his room through the sheer curtains. Normally, he woke with the sun. He liked to sleep and wake early. It just made his body and mind feel better to have something of a routine, but today, he felt so out of sorts, he didn't even know what time it was.

He could only imagine what it was like in the dungeons in constant darkness.

A soft knock at the door convinced him to finally sit up. His body ached despite having slept in his soft bed.

"Enter," he said.

The door was pushed open, and Sten entered, followed by one of the waitstaff pushing in a breakfast tray.

"Your highness," Sten said, nodding to him. "Your father requests your presence this morning."

Allard nodded, feeling oddly flat.

Yesterday, he would have died from the nerves, but he supposed, today he already knew how his parents felt about this. They knew he was married to a male now and they were most displeased... although, granted, so far, that seemed to be more because Fenian had forced the union.

"In his office?" he guessed, as his breakfast was left on the table at the window.

Sten clipped the curtains back, allowing bright rays of sunshine to flood the room.

"He's sitting in the garden, reading. He will wait until you are finished your breakfast."

Allard nodded.

"That will be all this morning," he said, dismissing his servant.

Sten's thick gray brow twitched in surprise, but he nodded and departed, sealing the door behind him and leaving Allard to his own thoughts once more.

He stood, washed his face, brushed his hair, and dressed. When he looked in the mirror, he looked like his usual self.

So much had changed that he was shocked he still looked so normal.

He wasn't hungry, so left the meal untouched, eager to hear what his father had to say about the matter.

The king was in the garden under a canopy, reading a book. He seemed to be waiting for Allard though because the moment he approached, he closed it and set it aside, and pushed to his feet.

"Walk with me," he said.

The friendly tone set Allard instantly on edge.

"What's the matter?" he asked. "Did something else happen?"

His father shook his head.

"Not at all. I just want to talk."

Not waiting for Allard's response, he waved off the footmen standing by, dismissing them, and put an arm around Allard's shoulders, leading him to the garden paths.

It was strange for them to walk together, even on a nice afternoon. They didn't do things like that. In fact, when Allard thought about it, they had very few *real* conversations that went beyond pleasantries or orders.

It would be wrong to say that his father was never kind to him, though. Their relationship was amicable, but that was mostly because he rarely, if ever, stepped out of line.

Allard always did as he was told. He lived up to the role of the perfect prince very well, and because of that, he was given the freedom to do the things he wanted, such as hunting.

It now occurred to Allard for the first time, that the only things he really liked to do involved being alone. What did that say about him and his actual happiness with his role as prince?

He sighed, wishing he could just shut off the unfortunate journey of self-discovery that he had been on since discovering his sexuality.

Now that Fenian was literally in his home—more like *under* it—he couldn't ignore his feelings any longer. Which, he supposed was the reason for his father's current mood.

"I suppose you want to talk about my marriage," he guessed, and his father flinched.

"You are not married," he said. "There was no ceremony."

"But a magic bond was made," Allard reminded him. "…and we consummated it."

He didn't know why he added that last part. He spared an anxious glance at his father's face. When he saw the pinched look and the clenched jaw, he got his answer. He supposed he'd wanted to know what his father thought about him being with a man since it hadn't been addressed. The fact that Allard wasn't remotely surprised by his father's reaction made him think he must be a masochist. Why even try unless he wanted to see proof of how disapproving his father was?

"About that," King Jareth said, still not looking at him. "The bond can be severed. We were informed that you were given that option immediately afterward, before even returning here."

Allard swallowed down the fear at the realization of where this conversation was going.

"I won't allow it," he said, firmly.

Immediately, his father stopped walking. He turned to face him.

"I'm afraid you have no choice. If we leave you attached to this criminal, the elves will be made to pay. If we break it now, no harm will come to anyone."

"Except Fenian."

"Are you defending him?!" the king demanded.

Allard was even though he knew he shouldn't. No matter what nonsense Fenian had been whispering all night, what he had done was still reprehensible.

"If the bond is reversed, I'll never be able to love again," he said.

"If it isn't, you'll remain enamored by the bastard who used you."

"He was desperate. Can't you understand? They were going to kill him."

There he went again, defending Fenian despite himself.

"Oh, I understand," King Jareth snarled. "He saw a *prince* and knew exactly how to take advantage of him for his own selfish gain. How convenient for *him*. From a cell to a castle!"

"Please," Allard laughed. "The elven prison cells are far more comfortable than ours are."

"Better that than your chambers."

Allard was done with this argument. He turned, ready to march away—which was quite a bold statement when it was the king he was snubbing, father or not.

"Wait."

His father's hand landed on his arm.

When Allard looked at him, he was breathing heavily, calmness returning to him. He even looked a little bit sympathetic.

"I'm sorry son," he said, "but I meant what I said. This bond is going to be reversed... We cannot risk unrest between our people and the elves. We share our land. And I cannot allow the kingdom to think I allowed my son to be taken advantage of. I am asking you to go along with it without fighting."

He squeezed Allard's shoulder as his heart plummeted.

"Maybe it won't be true love, but perhaps you'll develop strong feelings for your future wife."

With that, he offered Allard a small smile and released him, the conversation over.

Allard was shaking as he walked away. He didn't make it far, heading for a bench hidden by the hedges.

I can't take this.

The sudden words—Fenian's voice in his head, startled him... They were so in line with what Allard was thinking.

I should have let them kill me. I would have too if I'd known that instead, I would have to sit here and think.

Allard snorted, surprisingly amused by the elf's disgruntled tone. He could *so* relate.

I wonder what you *would think, Allard, if you knew what my crimes were...*

Allard held his breath, waiting. The frustrating conversation with his father faded from his mind. All that remained was this. Would Fenian tell him?

I find myself thinking back, Fenian said. *Like there is a long line of circumstances and choices that led to this moment. Once I was on this path, it was nearly impossible to get off it... I was a thief and... I killed someone, Allard.*

There was silence, following Fenian's confession. For a long time, Allard sat still, his hands shaking. Somehow, he hadn't expected that. Fenian was sneaky, yes, but a murderer?

I didn't see her in there. She wasn't supposed to get

hurt... All my life, I tried to justify my actions. I always tried to pass the blame. The truth is, I was the one in the wrong. I'm sorry I dragged you into my despair. For a moment, when we were together, life seemed glorious, did it not?

I've never truly felt like I belonged anywhere until then.

Fenian fell silent then and Allard stared unseeing at the wall of hedges before him.

The elf had just confessed to a murder and yet Allard had the deepest, most irrational desire to go to him.

The dungeons were known to bring even the hardest of men to their knees. It was a world of constant darkness and ice-cold discomfort.

Imagining the mysterious and dangerously attractive elf imprisoned there, falling into deep despair, seemed wrong.

He wanted to comfort him or even... to free him.

Allard shook the thought away. It wouldn't change anything.

It wasn't his choice for Fenian to be in the dungeons, and he wouldn't be able to free him. The guards followed the king's orders over Allard's.

Even if he *did* free Fenian, then what? Would they run off to a distant island and live with new identities? The idea was absurd. Allard couldn't abandon his current life for the person who had started their relationship on lies and betrayals.

But still, as Fenian continued to whisper deep, intimate thoughts into Allard's mind throughout the rest of the day, Allard could not resist the growing need to at least check on him.

He had to wait though. His mother wanted to have lunch with him, but he could scarcely even listen to her over Fenian's nearly constant whispering. Despite her worried gaze, he excused himself to his room just so he could pace the floor.

By evening, he sat by his window, staring over the horizon, the Green Veil in the distance, the ocean on the other side. But for him, the spectacular sunset was ruined by the fact that Fenian was in the dungeons in the pitch black, unable to see it.

He felt such a confusing number of conflicting emotions that it nearly made him sick.

Fenian had started to talk about him again, here and there words sprinkled in like; *your eyes, so pure,* and *the way I felt with you inside me,* had nearly killed him. Especially as they were mixed in with the strangest things. Things that pulled his heart and seemed to physically pain him. *Since my mother died, no one has ever looked at me like I was special. Not until that morning with you.* Then there was a rant, one filled with anger that only depressed Allard even more. *I shouldn't have done it! I knew I shouldn't! I was foolish enough to think that I would remain in control, but I'm not.* You *are in full control. You already own me, yet I know nothing about you, only that you drive me crazy and you left me here to rot! Well, the joke is on you and your mighty family because when I die down here, I will take you with me and we will* both *deserve it.*

Allard couldn't take much more of this. Dusk couldn't come fast enough.

The moment the sun was behind the horizon, he changed into something more inconspicuous, plain black clothes and boots, and then slipped from his room.

No one questioned him walking around the halls, after all, he was the prince. When he stepped out into the evening air, he kept close to the walls, seeking the shadows, eager to remain unseen.

As he neared the entrance to the dungeons, he saw the guard on duty there, leaning against the wall, glancing around in boredom.

Allard didn't blame him, it was a long, uneventful job. People didn't escape the dungeons, so there was rarely anything to do.

Allard sank back into the shadows, watching the man, waiting for his shift to end, praying it wouldn't be too long and that he'd be able to get inside without being seen.

He could march right up to the guard and tell him he was visiting, but he didn't want an escort and he didn't want his father to know.

He needed to talk to Fenian properly, to see his face and discuss what had happened between them.

His heart pounded against his ribs at the prospect of seeing his husband. No matter what his father believed, Allard couldn't help thinking of Fenian that way.

He didn't know what he was going to do, but now that he was staring at the darkened tunnel into the dungeon, he knew one thing; he would not rest until Fenian was free.

CHAPTER 13

FENIAN

Fenian rested his forehead on the cold metal. His body was oddly accustomed to the constant chill now. Of course, that didn't mean that he was comfortable here, far from it.

He had never been one who could handle stillness. He sought out movement, adventure... that was probably part of the reason he had always been a troublemaker. He'd never been able to sit and listen, the way his teachers wanted.

He sighed heavily, listening to the way small noises echoed over the damp walls. There was only dripping water and the scurrying of small rodents until another sound reached his ears. The shuffling almost sounded like it could be from a large animal.

Perhaps a large rat was arriving to give him some company. Fenian was so damn lonely that the idea was almost appealing. He really was going crazy in here.

I could do with some company, he said to Allard.

He'd been doing it all day; using inner speak directed at his husband. He couldn't help himself. Talking was all he had to do down here and the silent sounding board of Allard's presence seemed to be the only thing he had left.

If only we could talk in person, he sighed. *I would much prefer to see your face than these dirty walls. Where are you, my prince?*

"I'm here."

Fenian nearly jumped from his skin.

He spun in the direction of the voice and held out a hand, casting a sudden bright blue light in the direction it had come from.

The light was blinding to his eyes, now unaccustomed to the dark and he had to blink several times before he could make out Prince Allard's form as he crouched through the low entrance into Fenian's part of the dungeons.

He straightened then, squinting in Fenian's direction, trying to see him.

Fenian knew he should lower his hand and the intense light so that Allard could see him, but for a minute, he couldn't. Allard was a true vision. Dressed all in black, his golden hair disheveled and mud on his cheek from crawling through the tunnels, he took Fenian's breath away.

Swallowing, Allard came toward the bars and finally Fenian lowered his hand, casting the light on the floor. He shook a globe of blue free so that it floated around their feet, lighting them without him needing to hold onto it.

"What are you doing here?" Fenian asked, voice hoarse from disuse. "I don't suppose you've changed your mind on my sleeping arrangements, have you? I would still consider your bed if you asked nicely."

Allard didn't say anything. Fenian realized that he was unable to look at the human and that his gaze was instead fixed on the wall.

"Didn't you just say you wanted to see my face rather than the walls?" Allard asked. "I'm right here and now you won't look at me."

Frowning, he finally forced his gaze up to meet his husband's. His stomach somersaulted.

"You heard me. How...?"

"I heard everything," Allard confirmed.

Fenian stepped back, shock overwhelming him. For a moment, he felt so *exposed* that he couldn't breathe.

The light died, plunging them into darkness once more.

Shaking, Fenian took a shuddering breath.

"Fenian." Allard's soft voice broke the silence. "Come closer, please."

After countless hours in the pitch black, wishing for Allard, Fenian hesitated. He was afraid. Of what, he wasn't sure. Except that he hadn't known that Allard was listening, and he'd said so very much. What did the prince think of him?

"Please," Allard repeated.

Fenian heard him move and suddenly a hand brushed his arm. Allard was reaching through the bars blindly, trying to feel him and Fenian was suddenly powerless to fight him. He stepped forward, into Allard's outstretched hand, desperate for his touch.

His touch was so gentle that Fenian couldn't move as Allard stroked his arm lightly. His other hand brushed Fenian's cheek, then neck. Eventually, he settled with one hand clasping Fenian's, their fingers entwined, the other tangled in the hair at the nape of his neck. Allard seemed almost to be holding Fenian in place more than anything else and he couldn't help leaning against the touch.

For a while, all that existed was the sound of their breathing and the warmth of Allard's hands.

"Why did you come here?" Fenian finally asked.

"Because I couldn't take it," Allard whispered. "Knowing you were down here and hearing all the things you were saying... it was driving me mad."

"I didn't think you could hear me," Fenian admitted, his stomach clenching with nerves. He'd told Allard about his crimes and yet he was here, holding him.

"I assumed as much... I'm sorry. I know it wasn't really for my ears but there was nothing I could do."

Fenian snorted.

"I can't believe you would apologize to me for anything after what I did."

"I understand though," Allard said softly. "I wonder what I would do if I was about to be wrongly executed. What lengths would I take to save myself?"

"Wrongly?" Fenian asked, confused. "Allard... perhaps you missed the part where I said I killed someone. A young elf, *Sabina*."

He swallowed, wondering why he was suddenly so desperate to explain everything. Perhaps because, if Allard could accept all of him, even the worst parts, it would fix him somehow.

"You said it was an accident."

"The fire wasn't," Fenian breathed. His hands

started to shake, and Allard's fingers tightened, holding him still.

"I knew her... I didn't know she was in the shop and—"

Fenian swallowed. The words were stuck in his throat.

"You often started fires?" Allard asked.

Fenian nodded. In the dark, Allard couldn't see it, but he would feel it with the hand still on his neck.

He'd already told Allard most of this. He couldn't believe that all that time, Allard had been listening. Yet despite that, despite Fenian's angry breakdown and confession of murder, Allard was standing there, holding him, almost as though he wanted to comfort him.

"It was an accident," Allard said softly.

"I set that fire on purpose," Fenian argued. "She was young, with a family that loved her."

"And that makes her life more valuable than yours, I suppose?"

Fenian didn't have words. He knew the prince was probably overly sentimental because of their bond. Maybe Fenian was too. Maybe that was why it meant so much to him that Allard chose to take his side even though Fenian truly was not worth backing.

Gently, he reached up with his free hand,

through the bars until he found Allard. He traced his jaw and then his fingers found those soft lips that he had been dreaming of. He stroked them.

"This is just like our first meeting all over again," he whispered. "Me in a cell, you outside of it, close enough for me to touch. Or kiss… The only difference being that this time, we won't be interrupted, will we?"

Allard's breath hitched. It sounded loud in the silence. Instead of speaking, he shook his head. Suddenly, his lips parted, and he gently took the tip of Fenian's finger, sucking it.

Fenian's breath shuddered, a moan broke through his lips, and then they were reaching out wildly, grabbing each other.

The bars were in the way, but not enough to stop them. Their erect cocks met, and they ground together hungrily, moaning as their lips sealed together.

Their tongues tangled as they started thrusting, hands gripping each other's rears and pulling closer.

With a groan, Fenian dragged himself back, yanking his pants down. When he returned, desperate to be touched, Allard wasn't there.

He reached through the bars, finding him fumbling with his buttons.

"Light," Allard whispered desperately.

Fenian created another small blue orb, a dimmer one this time, that was just enough for Allard to see. Quickly, he pulled his pants open and pushed them down. Like Fenian, he didn't bother to remove them completely or he'd have to take his boots off too and there was no time for that.

Able to see the prince's fine body, his muscular thighs, and his hard cock, Fenian's cock hardened even more. He reached out, pushing Allard's shirt up so he could see more.

"You're gorgeous," he whispered.

"You too," Allard returned. And he *was* watching Fenian like he was a true work of art, despite the fact that he had spent however long in this muddy place. He couldn't look that great, but the way Allard reached out to touch him, almost reverently, sent a thrill through his body and made him feel like the most attractive person alive.

He gripped Fenian by the hip, pulling him to the bars again, and then pressed his own in as well, so that their lengths rutted together.

When he reached down, taking them in his hand together, Fenian's eyes rolled back.

Their foreheads pressed together, both watching as he stroked them, precum slicking their lengths.

Fenian's thighs were shaking. He tried to breathe through the incredible sensations, to hold back but this was Allard's hand and his cock and even that fact was too much for him.

Without warning, his hips jerked forward, and he started to come, gripping the bars to keep himself up as his cock pumped and strained into Allard's fist, covering both of their lengths in the slick liquid.

Allard groaned, continuing to pump as he watched, enthralled.

"Do you want to fuck me again?" Fenian asked, still breathless.

Allard looked barely capable of forming sentences, his gaze so hazy with desire, his face flushed red, but he managed to nod and order with a shaky breath, "turn around."

Fenian did.

He pressed his backside to the bars and gripped his knees to keep himself up. He was still trembling from the strength of his orgasm, but he wanted more. He wanted to keep going all night.

"Fuck me," he whispered encouragingly, and Allard made a desperate noise behind him, gripping his hips and lining his tip with Fenian's entrance.

With a shuddering breath, he pushed.

They both moaned as he was entered. It was a bit painful without any preparation, but Allard's cock was wet with cum and Fenian just didn't care. The stretching pain made him focus on the here and now so much that he may as well have been meditating. There was nothing but Allard pushing into him, pressing deeper and then deeper still. His sweet, pleasured gasps and sighs echoed around them, and it was the best Fenian had felt in a long time. Like he was useful. Like he was *good.*

"*Oh,*" Allard moaned, starting to thrust. He pumped his hips into Fenian's backside, pulled back, and then pressed in, another fluid motion as he drew out, almost to the tip, and then filled him again.

A few more deep strokes like that and Fenian was hard again, moaning in time with the thrusts, and then, when Allard picked up speed, fucking him hard, his moans turned to a nearly constant, incoherent cry of pleasure.

Their voices echoed, probably to the exit but Fenian half wanted someone to come to see this— only if they weren't going to interrupt. How delightful would that be, for all to know that the human prince wanted to fuck him so badly he'd do it through a set of prison bars.

His hips smacked into them stopping his movements, but he pulled Fenian back with each thrust, so his cock still reached deep inside, and then, suddenly his thrusts became erratic.

Warmth suddenly erupted inside him. Allard kept

going though, groaning while he continued to pump into Fenian, his hole now wet and loose.

Finally, with a deep sigh, Allard pulled out, releasing him.

For a moment, Fenian was unsure what would happen next. Allard had gotten his release. Fenian had too. Although he wanted another one, there was no reason for Allard to stay... except, he didn't seem eager to go yet, because he reached through the bars again, pulling Fenian's back to them and moaning while he started to feel his backside, fingers tracing the wet spill of his seed on Fenian's hole.

Allard's hand brushed his hard cock and he stilled for a moment then gently gripped Fenian's length with a soft gasp.

"Hard again," he said in awe.

Fenian chuckled breathlessly.

"I couldn't help it," he said. "You were too good."

"Oh fuck," Allard breathed. "Do you want more?"

Without waiting, he pressed a finger inside Fenian, moaning as though it was his length again.

Fenian bit his lip and allowed his head to fall back against the bars.

"Keep going," he begged.

At once, Allard started to stroke his length, fingers delving inside him at the same time, first one, then two.

He started to pump them within him, stroking at the same time until Fenian's entire body clenched tightly, and he came, clinging to the bars behind him, sure that he was about to fall.

The moment his shuddering orgasm faded, he did, slipping to the ground in a heap.

Prince Allard came down with him, arms still around him.

For a long time, they sat like that, leaning close together.

Eventually, the small dim light went out and they remained in darkness, still holding onto each other's arms.

When Allard eventually shifted, Fenian knew what was coming at once.

"Don't go."

Allard paused.

"I'll come back."

Fenian nearly choked.

"You can't just leave me down here to visit whenever you want to get off," he spat.

A long silence rang. When Allard finally spoke, it was not in anger like Fenian had expected. He didn't rise to the bait.

First, his hand found Fenian's again, squeezing it and Fenian nearly cried because Allard knew. He somehow just *knew* that Fenian lashed out without meaning to. That it came from fear.

"I'm going to take you out of here," he whispered. "But I can't do it now—"

"Why not?"

"I don't have the key, for one."

When Allard released him and stood, Fenian scrambled to his feet, eyes straining even though he knew there was no way to see anything down here.

He heard him moving, the shuffling of clothes, and then fabric touched him.

Fenian took it, curiously.

"What is it?" he asked.

"My cloak," Allard said. "It's cold down here…"

Fenian's fingers clutched the fabric. Irrationally, he wanted to cling onto Allard, to keep him there with him.

"Stay a little longer," he begged. When there was no answer, he added. "Please, stay. Let me suck your cock."

Allard let out a breath.

"Where are you?" he muttered and Fenian could hear him step closer.

He reached out blindly, and they found each other at once.

Relief swept through him as Allard gripped his face and pressed a deep kiss to his lips.

When he eventually pulled back, he didn't go far, remaining close enough that their lips brushed when he spoke.

"I'm going to try to get you out of here the right way," he whispered, "and if that doesn't work, I'm breaking you out. Tomorrow night. Can you wait that long?"

Fenian swallowed.

"How do I know you'll be back?"

"Because I promise."

"But—"

"I always keep my promises."

Fenian squeezed his eyes shut, trying to force calmness. He found it hard to trust most of the time, now was no different.

"If only I could speak to you, the way you do to me."

"I thought it would work with our bond," Fenian sighed. "But I couldn't hear you at all."

"How do you do it?"

"You didn't hear my instructions?" Fenian asked, surprised.

Allard shook his head.

"For a few hours, you were coming in and out before it was really clear."

Hope bubbling within him, Fenian explained.

"Close your eyes and envision my face," he began.

"Then as though you are speaking to me, direct your words at me silently."

For a long moment, there was silence.

Fenian... you make me feel unlike I ever have before.

Fenian smiled, heart soaring.

You too, Prince.

Allard took a steadying breath, pressed a quick kiss to Fenian's lips, and backed away before Fenian could try to stop him again.

He reached out, but his hand met cold, damp air as the sound of footsteps retreating filled the small corridor.

Tomorrow night, Allard promised, and was gone, leaving Fenian, once more to his thoughts and utter loneliness.

CHAPTER 14

SENECA

Seneca tapped the folded sheet of paper on the table, his gaze fixed on the clouds above. The other members of the council were seated around him but for the first time Seneca could recall, true silence stretched between them.

After the events that had transpired, and hours of heated debate, they were at a standstill.

"I must say," Yana said, suddenly breaking the silence, "I agree with Seneca."

Seneca appreciated Yana's support. She was the eldest of the group of them and although they voted on all their decisions, her opinion held weight.

"Explain why?" Elli asked. "I'm finding it difficult

to go back on our decision. Especially after the added offense of forcing a bond on a human."

"It is exactly because of the human that I've changed my mind," Yana said. "He sees something in Fenian. He defends him despite everything."

"Of course," Kial snorted. "He is bound to him."

"Fenian is not all bad," Seneca said. "He was an innocent child once, just as we all were."

"And we all did not become dangerous criminals," Kial pointed out.

Seneca couldn't argue that.

"When he was young, he sought guidance. I was too busy for him when he needed me."

"And now you have a bleeding heart when days ago you were willing to watch his execution."

Kial's cutting words affected Seneca more deeply than he let show. For years he had practiced patience and focus, never allowing anything personal to interfere with his position in life. Serving the community and the council was all he had left.

They were seated, as they often were, in the back patio of the local restaurant they frequented, and before he could respond, the back door opened.

Normally, they went there when difficult matters had been settled, but sometimes, such as in this case, it was because they could not come to an agreement and needed a break in business to clear their minds.

All five of them were completely silent as the food was brought outside, but Seneca could not stop himself from speaking to his comrades, Kial in particular.

Fenian fought to survive with all of his being. Perhaps because somewhere deep inside himself, he knew that we were in the wrong, that Sabina—

This isn't about Sabina, Kial snapped.

Oh, but it is. It is unjust for Fenian to be executed for murdering someone whom we all know, still lives.

He is right, Nellis suddenly added. *Like Seneca, I was following the majority. Now... I feel guilt for even allowing it to go this far. In a way, we are all responsible for this current situation.*

Seneca looked at his comrade, shocked. They had both agreed to something against their better judgment. They shouldn't have let the more forceful of the group do all the arguing.

Elli though, who always worked closely with Kial, rolled her eyes.

Why is it that now, *the three of you are against this? Now that we may be attacked by the human army if we do not sever the bond?*

Because it is the right thing to do, Yana said.

We have been pushed into a corner, Kial argued. *We must sever the bond and then, if you still disagree with the execution, we can resume the discussion.*

Seneca shook his head, unwilling to be pushed into a corner again. He could not take part in this a second time, especially not with the added blow of a forced bond severance.

You know I was against it initially, but once the decision had been made, my loyalty went to you, Kial. That is why I backed your decision all this time, despite how difficult it has been for me.

Finally, food set on their table, the restaurant staff departed, and Seneca leaned toward his friend, meeting his hard, obsidian gaze.

"All I ask is that you support me in this, the way I have supported you."

Another long silence rang between them and then, to his great disappointment, Kial shook his head.

"You have my deepest respect Seneca, but we cannot forget that letter."

He indicated the one still held in Seneca's hand and Elli nodded somberly.

"He is correct. We are being held responsible for this."

"Because it *is* our fault," Seneca argued.

She shrugged loosely.

"Whether or which, we cannot simply do *nothing*. The human king should not be completely ignored. Severing the bond is the simplest way to fix this situation."

"We have argued enough for the day," Yana cut in. "Think over one another's opinions with an open mind and then we will revisit this issue in the morning. In the meantime, let us eat."

The others turned to the food, content to follow Yana's instructions but Seneca had no appetite.

For a moment, he sat stiffly, unsure what to do.

He'd honestly thought that his word would mean more to his comrades. He'd thought his opinion carried more weight. As it stood, he was unsure how to stop the bond from being cut on his own.

ALLARD

ALLARD'S FEET tapped the marble floors under the table nervously.

He hadn't slept a wink. After spending most of the night with Fenian, it had just felt wrong to lay in a comfortable bed while he was down there on the cold, hard ground.

Instead, he'd planned at length what to say to his father. He had something of a speech now rehearsed, but he was still afraid of what would be said. If his parents were like the king and queen of Suvhal, they would eventually come around. Even better, if Tasnia was anything like Casetro, he could love whomever he liked and would not be judged for it.

But he was not from Casetro. His friend Nikolai had always been so free and fun, perhaps that was part of the reason.

Sighing, Allard shook the thought away just as the doors were opened and his father strode into the breakfast hall, his mother just behind him.

"Oh, Allard. You're joining us today?"

She seemed delighted to see him. Even his father patted him on the shoulder as he passed to sit at the chair at the head of the table.

He nodded, having to physically swallow down the fear that rose up his throat in the form of bile.

Get it together, he told himself.

"Did you sleep well?" his mother asked, sitting across from him.

Allard cleared his throat and nodded, then shook his head.

"Not really," he admitted. "I was up most of the night."

"Overthinking," his father said, shaking his head. "You always had that problem, son."

"Perhaps."

Just then, breakfast was wheeled in, and platters

laid before them, so Allard bit his lip, waiting for the right moment.

They began to eat in relative silence. His mother kept the chit-chat going, asking pointless questions, remarking on things of so little interest it was hard to even play along. When she started talking about the roses in the garden, Allard finally broke.

"About Fenian," he interrupted.

A silence fell over the room and Allard instantly regretted speaking. He hadn't meant to jump into it so ineloquently.

His father took a bit of bread, chewing slowly while he watched him.

He was waiting for Allard to say more, but he knew his father well enough to know that the king was already on guard, ready to argue.

He tried to remember his speech, the points of his argument that he had agonized over.

"I was thinking about the situation," he began.

"Well, that's the problem, isn't it?" his father asked. "As I said, you think too much. Don't worry about it, I will take care of everything."

Allard gripped the edge of the table and forced himself on as though he hadn't been interrupted.

"It's not the best situation, but as you know, I am not willing to have the bond reversed at this time."

His voice was trembling the slightest bit. He took a small breath and forced it to level before continuing.

"You wanted to strengthen our alliance with the elves," he said. "Perhaps this is a blessing in disguise. After all, I find myself married to one now—"

Suddenly, the king's hands smacked down on the table with a bang. The dishes rattled and his mother squealed in surprise.

As everything settled, she stared at her husband with wide eyes, hand over her heart.

Allard's was racing too as he stared at his father, who was glaring daggers at him.

"You are *not* married," he said slowly. "How many times must I say it? No son of mine would be permitted to wed a male *or* an elf."

Allard drew back.

He couldn't find the words to argue.

"He didn't mean it," his mother said, softly. "Let it go, dear."

But shock grew to fury in Allard at her words.

"I *did* mean it," he said. "It may not have been a human wedding, but it was more than that. Our *souls* are bound and by keeping Fenian in that dungeon, part of me is down there with him."

His mother let out a distressed noise.

"That's why we will reverse the bond," his father said, almost like it was meant to comfort them. "We will inform the elves that you will go ahead with it and then you will forget about this whole ordeal soon."

Why was his father refusing to believe that the effects would linger on forever? He'd been told more than once. Not wanting to get hung up on that detail, Allard focused on the more pressing one.

"What if I don't want to forget it?"

"Excuse me?"

"Fenian will be executed. I don't want that. I—I care about him."

"Enough."

Suddenly, his father pushed to his feet.

"The decision has been made. I already sent word. Seneca will return with the bond breaker by morning."

Allard shook his head, but his father chose not to wait around for more arguments. He stormed from the room, leaving a stunned Allard sitting numbly at the breakfast table.

"You shouldn't have said that," his mother said.

"What?"

"That you care about him. It's hard enough knowing *how* the bond was consummated..."

Allard's cheeks heated. He pushed the thoughts of the previous night firmly from his mind.

"Does it matter?" he asked.

She shifted uneasily.

"Well, of course, it does, love. It's not natural. He's a male…"

"You can't really feel that way. You invited Nemir and Soluc into our home. You hosted their wedding!"

"Yes, but Prince Nemir is not our child, is he? And Soluc is our subject. It was a very fortuitous union for us, really. If the Suvahl royal family doesn't mind their son marrying a male, then that's up to them. We wouldn't interfere with the personal lives of our allies."

Allard felt queasy. With it all finally laid out on the table, he didn't know how to feel except tired and disappointed.

"So, like father, you would prefer me to be in a loveless marriage, to never feel love ever again."

"It's more than that," she said, frowning. "You're our only son, Allard. Don't we need heirs?"

Allard didn't know what to say to that. It had already crossed his mind that they wouldn't have children together.

"Not to mention the fact that he's a criminal and he forced you into this," she added. "He's not good enough for you, Allard."

"Well, he may be my only choice."

Allard pushed up from the table but paused and looked at his mother.

"And I'm glad that he is," he added. "I like him. I did even before the bond."

He walked away, slightly mollified by the look of shock on her face.

Fenian, are you awake?

He asked as he walked. He waited with bated breath for a reply. They had both been silent since his departure and he hoped desperately that his voice would be heard.

Yes, Allard. Awake and thinking of you.

His response set Allard's heart racing. All the tension from the conversation he'd had with his parents evaporated.

They won't release you. We can't stay here, he said. *We must run tonight.*

There was a long silence, then Fenian's soft voice.

I'll be waiting.

CHAPTER 15

FENIAN

*T*he sun is setting.

Prince Allard's voice speaking quietly in his mind was like a soothing balm.

Fenian gripped the icy bars to ground himself.

What does it look like?

Beautiful. The sky is orange, the sun is reflecting off the ocean as it sets. Above, the clouds have turned purple. It all seems so vast. Like nothing in our small world really matters.

Allard's apt description made Fenian smile.

I wish I was watching it with you, Fenian said.

Soon, Allard promised. *No matter where we end up, at least we'll always have the sunsets.*

Fenian's stomach fluttered.

Allard certainly seemed like he meant it. He was actually going to leave everything he knew for *Fenian,* of all people. And Fenian was waiting. Wrapped up in Allard's warm cloak, he knew he was in over his head. He knew they were bonded now, that there was a certain understanding between them, but still, Fenian didn't know how he had ever become so lucky.

Even if Allard later decided that he couldn't do it, that Fenian wasn't worth it, the fact that he was even going to *try* meant everything to him.

What are you doing now? he asked, curious after a stretch of silence.

Going to the stables, then coming to you. I timed the guard's shift change last time. I'll sneak in, but once you are free, we will have to move fast.

Fenian swallowed.

He stood, stretched, and couldn't help beginning to pace.

Back and forth he walked around his cell, ducking his head in the low spots where he needed to.

It's getting dark now, Allard whispered. *I can see the guard. He's bored out of his mind and barely paying attention. It will only be a minute.*

Again, the silence stretched.

Now! Allard shouted to him.

Are you in? Fenian asked anxiously.

A minute passed and then, a shuffling noise echoed to him and Allard's stooped form, shrouded in a long cloak, crouched into view.

He straightened as soon as he could, grinning as his eyes fell on Fenian and coming to him, his arms outstretched.

Fenian took them, trying to embrace his lover as his heart leaped. A laugh burst from his lips.

"Hurry up and open this damn door so I can hold you properly."

Allard laughed breathlessly and reached for the pouch strung around his hips.

"I had no clue how to get the key," he admitted, "but I took a leaf out of your book and got this instead."

He held it open so that Fenian could see the white powder within.

"Explosive powder," he explained. "If we put it in the lock, can you light it?"

Fenian grinned.

"Brilliant thinking."

Kneeling, Allard scooped the powder out, pushing as much as he could into the small hole.

Fenian held his light out for him to see what he was doing until finally, he sat back on his heels with a helpless shrug.

"That's the best I can do."

"Stand back," Fenian ordered, eyeing the powder that still coated Allard's hands and had fallen across his cloak.

Allard did, not stopping until his back was flat against the opposite wall.

Fenian allowed his small light to diffuse to nothing and concentrated. Worried as he was about making a fire that was too large, one that might catch Allard somehow, he took his time, focusing all his energy on the little keyhole.

The moment he even thought of the spell, a bright light burst from it. The explosion lit the darkness, blinding him, metal went flying, hitting the walls around them.

The crash echoed around them and seemed to reverberate the entire castle.

Allard yelped in surprise and then they were plunged once more into darkness.

For a moment, there was only the sound of their breathing.

"Did—did it work?" Allard asked.

Fenian reached forward, tentatively. His fingers found the door. It was sitting at an angle, *open.*

Happiness burst in him, brighter than the explosion he'd caused, and without hesitating, he shoved the door out of the way, not caring as it crashed to the ground and went toward where Allard had been standing.

The moment his hands touched Allard, he released a shuddering breath and pushed into Fenian's arms.

They both laughed, relieved, clinging to each other.

Allard's chest was rising and falling rapidly. He pressed his face into Fenian's neck and held on so tightly that Fenian felt it in his heart. A squeezing of *something* that was so damn tender, he didn't know how to handle it.

"We should go," Allard whispered. "Someone *must* have heard that."

He didn't let go through. His grip tightened.

"Are you afraid?" Fenian asked.

After a long moment of stillness, Allard nodded.

"I'm sure they'll come after us but, it's not that... I'm leaving my home tonight. Probably permanently."

"You don't have to," Fenian whispered, even though his very being protested them being apart. For Allard to give up his position as a *prince* just seemed wrong.

Allard shook his head though.

"I won't send you off without me," he said. "I don't want that either."

He shook himself and pulled back, taking Fenian's hand and holding it tightly.

"I've made my decision. Let's go."

They had to release each other to get through the passageway. It was hard enough to crawl through without clinging to one another.

Masochists must have made this place, Fenian said silently. *It's just as unpleasant for the captor as it is for the prisoner.*

Allard snorted.

"I doubt that," he whispered back. "Normally, we wouldn't even come down here. Exploring the place as a child and having the life scared out of me by one of the prisoners was enough to turn me off the place for good… It's inhumane."

"Is that why no one else is kept here?"

"Actually, people *are* kept here short term. It's a bit too old world now for long sentences. There's another prison to the south. More modern."

More like the elven prison? Fenian asked, reverting to inner speak as they neared the exit.

Not really, Allard said. *It's still enclosed, just not underground.*

Fenian shuddered.

The human prisons were completely unnatural and cruel.

As one, they slowed as they neared the exit. The

corridor was high enough to stand in but just as damp as the rest of the place.

Allard pressed back against him, pushing him into the shadows.

Together, they remained still, waiting.

Fenian tilted his head, trying to see around Allard, unable to help to note how nice his hair smelled as it tickled his nose.

He'd bedded many people in his life, but Fenian could honestly say, he had never wanted to hold someone close simply for the pleasure of their near-ness. Yet that was what he wanted to do with Prince Allard more than anything.

He wanted to embrace him and breathe him in, feel his warmth and not think of anything else.

Come on, Allard whispered silently.

Fenian followed as he started to move, but stopped, realizing that the guard was still standing in front of the entrance, his back turned toward them.

Looks like we were lucky. It must not have been as loud an explosion as we thought.

What are you doing? Fenian demanded as Allard crept ever closer.

We don't have any other choice.

And with that ominous statement, he jumped from the cave's entrance and straight onto the knight.

He fell with a shout, ready to fight, but Allard already had the man flat on his stomach, his wrists behind his back. He tied them tightly with rope from his pack and then gagged the man with fabric that Fenian hadn't even seen him procure. He'd been planning this.

The man struggled furiously, grunting, trying to flip over to see who his assailant was, but they didn't give him the chance. They took off into the night.

The fresh, dry air was nearly enough to make Fenian cry.

Above him, the stars seemed to be brighter than he'd ever seen them before. The flickering lights shone down on them, illuminating their path as they hurried in silence, hands clasped.

The world was beautiful, Fenian thought. Allard was too. Inside and out and Fenian was overwhelmingly grateful that he was still here to be a part of it all.

CHAPTER 16

ALLARD

*T*his *way*, Allard said, leading Fenian toward the barns.

He'd left his mare around the corner, tied up and waiting. She was the only thing he was taking with him aside from the clothes on his back and a small pack of supplies, and Fenian, of course. That was his most valuable steal.

His hand squeezed the elf's as they rounded the corner, finding Blossom waiting patiently.

Fenian paused as Allard climbed swiftly atop her.

You're really planning to leave with me, aren't you?

Allard looked down at Fenian. In the dim light of the night, he could just make out the look of awe on his face. Fenian hadn't really believed it, it seemed.

Allard couldn't blame him. By the sounds of it, Fenian had never had anyone on his side before.

It would take time to convince him that he was worth leaving home for, but Allard was more than willing to put in the hours.

He reached down, taking Fenian's hand, and helped him up behind him.

His thighs were warm around Allard's.

When Fenian wrapped his arms around his waist, in more of a hug than a need for stability, Allard couldn't help taking a moment to lean back against his strong chest.

They didn't have time to waste though, so as much as he wanted to turn and kiss Fenian and hold onto him, he nudged his horse forward, easing her onto the path that would take them away from the castle, and the town.

Fenian didn't seem to mind. He rested his chin on Allard's shoulder and held onto him tightly, not saying a word for over an hour.

"Where are we going?" he asked.

Allard was surprised to hear a note of tension in his voice. Then he realized, they were entering the Green Veil. The trees immediately blotted out the stars, but Allard could just make out the path. It was the fastest way on land to get out of Tasnia, but to Fenian's distrustful nature, it probably seemed like Allard was taking him back to the elves.

He reached down, placed a hand over Fenian's where it still rested on his waist, and gently stroked a thumb over his knuckles.

"I don't believe I can stay in Tasnia," he said gently. "No matter where we go, my family will track us down and bring us home."

"Then where will we go?"

"Casetro," he answered, heart skipping. "No one will know us and couplings like ours are accepted there... we can start a life together."

Fenian's grip on him tightened.

The breath he took against Allard's back trembled.

Suddenly, he kissed Allard's neck.

It was just a gentle press of lips to his skin, but it went straight through Allard's body, instantly setting it aflame.

He moaned softly, head tilting to give his lover more access.

Fenian took it eagerly, kissing and sucking the skin there until Allard was fully hard.

Fenian's hands splayed open against his abdomen, one slipped lower, pressing against his erection through his clothes. He groaned.

"Can't we stop for a few minutes?"

He pressed forward, grinding his own hard cock against Allard's backside with a shuddering breath.

Allard shook his head while his whole body protested.

"There's no time," he breathed. "We have to cross the border into Casetro before they have a chance to catch up to us."

"How long until the guard change at the dungeon?" he asked. "We have until then before it's even known that we are gone, right?"

He began to stroke Allard through his clothes.

"We don't have to stop," Allard whispered.

Fenian's grip on him tightened and he let out a breathy chuckle.

"Are you that eager for me?" he asked.

Allard nodded, leaning back into his embrace, heart racing, desperate for more.

"Oh no, my prince," Fenian sighed. "I let you have your fun with my body twice already. This time, it's my turn and I won't be able to fuck you the way I want to on the back of a horse."

Allard swallowed, mouth going dry as Fenian rubbed his length, thrusting gently against his backside while he did.

Allard tried to resist. Truly, he did, yet he couldn't stop himself from grinding back into that hard length, shuddering with pleasure at the very *idea* of being entered.

Twice now, he'd been inside Fenian, and it had been incredible, but he couldn't help wondering what it would feel like the other way around.

Fenian had seemed to enjoy it. He'd been hard as marble, moaning obscenely as he rode him the first time. The second time, braced against the bars, he'd been just as enthusiastic.

If not for the fact that Fenian had been in too much of a rush the first time, Allard would have been on the receiving end.

He'd considered that incredibly considerate from the person who happened to be stealing his freedom at the time. Although he had almost no hard feelings toward Fenian now, he was suddenly resentful of the fact he'd been robbed of the experience of having the elf's long shaft inside him.

He gripped the reins tightly, aggravated by Fenian's touch teasing him, keeping him hard as they rode.

After what felt like an eternity, he finally pulled Allard's pants open, freeing his length, now so hard it nearly hurt.

He took him in a firm grip and stroked him from base to tip. Just as a groan left his lips, thighs beginning to tremble, suddenly the touch was gone, leaving him straining in the cool night air.

Allard took a shuddering breath as the frustrating touches began again, first a gentle brush of fingers, so sensual that his whole body twitched, then a hard stroke, then—*nothing.* Allard's length strained; his body felt so on edge that he couldn't take it. He was so frustrated that tears stung his eyes.

And *again*, just as he thought that Fenian wasn't so evil, after all, he was proved wrong, very wrong, as Fenian stopped touching him just before his release. This was the most wicked person he had ever known.

"Why are you doing this?" he gasped.

Perhaps it was the tone of his voice that surprised Fenian, the obvious way it hitched with emotion was hard, even for him to ignore.

Either way, Fenian froze, then suddenly reached for Allard's chin, tilting his face back toward him to look into his eyes.

Allard could scarcely make eye contact. Tears burned a trail down his cheeks.

"Oh, Allard," Fenian breathed.

Suddenly, he kissed him deeply. It was so tender, so *loving* that Allard found it hard to believe this was the same person currently torturing him.

"I'm sorry," Fenian finally murmured. "I was just playing."

"Playing?" Allard demanded. "It's pure evil, what you're doing to me."

He sounded like a petulant child, but Fenian kissed him again, calming some of his frayed nerves.

"I wanted to convince you to get off this bloody animal," he sighed.

"Manipulating me. *Again*," Allard accused.

Fenian chuckled.

"Can you blame me?" he asked, suddenly gripping Allard's cock tightly. "You're so fun to tease. And anyway, this is just as painful for me."

He pressed into Allard's backside again, letting him feel his hard cock, and moaned softly. The sound went straight to Allard's shaft and a bead of liquid spilled from the tip. He shuddered.

"I want you so much," Fenian whispered into his ear. "I can barely take it."

Allard sagged, allowing the horse to slow, but not letting her stop completely.

"If we get down…"

"I'll make you come like you never have before."

Fenian's words, while his hand was still grasping Allard's length, were unbearable.

He practically jumped off the mare's back.

Fenian followed, just as eagerly.

He pulled Allard into his arms, kissing him so ravenously that his knees nearly gave out.

His pants were already undone, hanging loose around his hips and Fenian gripped the fabric, shoving it down, exposing him in the middle of the path to the night air, the elements, and whoever else happened by. And Allard didn't give a damn.

"I wanted to lay you down on a soft, comfortable bed and take my time having my way with you," Fenian said, "but the forest leaves will have to do."

Allard pulled back.

"Wait."

He went to the horse, nearly tripping over his pants, kicking them off in the process, and opened the bag strapped to her back. He'd been expecting at least a night outdoors once they reached Casetro and had brought *some* supplies.

Finding the rolled-up bundle, he pulled it free and held it out to Fenian.

"This should help," he said.

Fenian took it and pulled Allard off the path before finding a spot to spread the blanket out for them to lay on.

Once it was as even as it would get, he stepped up to Allard and slowly undressed him the rest of the way.

"Lay down," he instructed.

Allard did as he was told, spreading out on the blanket, shivering under Fenian's gaze.

Slowly, Fenian undressed, never breaking eye contact.

Allard couldn't look away. He wished that it was brighter, that he could see more of him, but anything was better than the dungeons had been, and he was grateful for every moment they were able to be alone together. Until now, they'd had to fight for nearly every moment they'd had in each other's presence.

Finally, they were alone, and they had some time.

Allard didn't care where they were anymore, only that they were there together.

When Fenian lowered down, he didn't climb atop Allard, the way he wanted him to. He was so eager to be embraced, to feel the elf's body, but instead, Fenian sat on his knees by Allard's legs, urging them apart.

He allowed his legs to be spread and waited, holding his breath as Fenian settled between them, gently stroking his thighs and stomach, neglecting his erection once again.

"I thought you were done teasing me," Allard said.

"I am."

With that, his fingers dropped lower, gently

caressing Allard's hole. He took his length in his other hand *finally*, but only held it as he deftly explored his entrance.

Allard tried to breathe through his nerves, but it didn't work. Fenian's hands felt nice, but he was so exposed. It was all so intimate, but Allard somehow felt alone.

"Fenian," he whispered. "Can't you kiss me?"

The elf's gaze shot up to meet Allard's, surprise in his eyes and without a moment wasted, he climbed up his body, draped himself over Allard's, and kissed him deeply.

Allard sighed in relief, arms wrapping around the elf to keep him there.

He'd wanted to try being on the receiving end, but he hadn't accounted for how *scary* it would feel. He couldn't do it.

He parted the kiss to say just that, but it was right at the moment that Fenian's hard tip suddenly stroked his hole and all that came out was a gasp.

He clenched and shivered, surprised by how nice the sensation was.

Fenian took Allard's face in his hands, holding him in place and pressing their lips together again. Gently, he began to thrust his hips, stroking Allard's entrance with his shaft until the feeling was overwhelming, leaving Allard somehow desperate for more.

"Let me touch you now," Fenian whispered. *Trust me, Allard. I will make you feel so good.*

Allard couldn't argue with that. He already *did* feel incredible. With the right touch now, he would probably come a little too easily. Liquid was already seeping from his tip, his hard length bobbing, desperate to be touched.

When Fenian reached down this time, he kissed Allard's chest, licking his hardened nipples while his finger played in the precome decorating his belly and his cock.

Then, Fenian used that to wet his hole and gently delved a finger into him. It slid in easily and felt foreign for only a moment. As soon as he started to move, gently stroking within him, it started to feel pleasant.

He sighed, legs falling further apart and Fenian kissed his way lower still.

He spent an agonizing moment, stroking him from within while his tongue licked down his length, and then he went past his cock, sucking Allard's soft skin all the way down until he reached his hole.

Allard shuddered as Fenian started to lick him there, pressing his tongue in around his finger, gently sucking the skin around it and generally, making Allard feel like he had never had any true intimacy in his life because this went beyond anything he'd experienced.

Having Fenian inside him, for no other purpose than to make him feel good was so overwhelming that once more, tears suddenly stung his eyes.

He gripped the blanket under him, trying desperately to ground himself, to hold on, but his thighs were already twitching, pressure and pleasure building inside him.

With long strokes of his tongue, Fenian was licking him, from hole to cock, all the way up to the tip and then back down again, finger thrusting within him, and Allard could take it no longer. He came suddenly, and with a cry, splattering his chest as his hips lifted off the ground and Fenian paused in his thrusting, pushing his finger in deep and pressing just where Allard needed it so that his orgasm kept coming for what felt like forever until it dwindled slowly and he was left limp, chest heaving, feeling weak... and then Fenian started again.

"What are you doing?" Allard gasped.

"We're not done yet," Fenian murmured, kissing his inner thigh. He sucked the skin there, just at the crease but didn't move closer to his softening cock for a moment, only continuing to leisurely stroke within him. Then, while Allard was too relaxed to properly argue, he eased another finger inside and gripped the base of his waning erection firmly, just holding it still.

"I said I would take my time having my way with you," Fenian reminded him. "I said I would make you come like you never had, didn't I?"

Allard swallowed, watching him, pretty sure that he was now married to an evil sex maniac and not about to complain.

"You did," he agreed.

Fenian smiled a truly wicked smile that went straight to Allard's cock, making it twitch unexpectedly. Then, he eased himself forward, spreading his knees and sliding his thighs under Allard's. He lined his tip with his entrance.

With a steadying hand on each of Allard's thighs now draped open over his legs, he pushed into him.

Allard's body began to tighten, but before it could, Fenian breached his entrance, sinking deep into him, stretching him beyond what he had been ready for.

A gasp tore through his throat. His fingers clutched the fabric under him. For a moment, he remained stiff, every muscle clenched.

Then, Fenian gripped his length and began to stroke it, coaxing pleasure back into Allard's body. Gentle, patient, and unrelenting.

He kept going, massaging Allard's cock until his body started to relax.

"That's it," Fenian breathed.

He began to move, barely at first, only a little wiggle of his hips until, eventually, like his finger before, it didn't feel uncomfortable anymore.

The pressure was oddly satisfying within him, the way it pressed into the back of his genitals from within, even the stretch of skin was somehow becoming pleasurable the longer Fenian was in him, swishing his hips in a gentle dance.

Finally, with a heavy sigh, Fenian leaned forward, bracing his hands on the fabric on each side of Allard's ribs.

"You're ready for more," he whispered. "I can tell, and quite frankly, I've been patient enough. If I don't start fucking you properly now, I might just die."

A breathy laugh left Allard.

"I believe we've been trying to avoid that," he agreed and then added silently, because it was too hard to say aloud, *Fuck me, Fenian.*

Groaning, Fenian started to move, sliding into him with long deep thrusts, promptly followed by deep grinding that made Allard's toes curl.

Fenian had been right. He *was* ready. Whatever he'd thought it would feel like, this was so much more than that. It felt so incredibly good that Allard thought he might come without even having his cock touched and then, Fenian shifted back, gripping his knees and started to go faster, his cock hitting Allard just where he had been stroking with his fingers earlier, and the pleasure he had been feeling increased tenfold.

"Fuck," he groaned, unable to think of anything more coherent than that or the cries bursting from his lips.

It was too much, too good. Too overwhelming.

With a cry, Allard started to come, his hole clenching spasmodically around the thick cock within it and Fenian's thrusts went off rhythm. He groaned and pushed on, filling Allard with a sudden burst of warmth until the last aftershocks of pleasure went through his body.

With a last deep thrust and heavy moan, Fenian pressed deeply into him one more time, stilling.

For a long moment, neither of them moved as their chests heaved for air.

When Fenian pulled out, Allard's body shuddered. It was shocking how something that had initially felt so intrusive could so quickly feel natural.

Almost as natural as the feeling of Fenian's arms as they wrapped around him. The strength in his biceps, the softness of his skin, his sure hands, were all so soothing and relaxing that Allard's eyes drooped despite the urgency of their situation.

"How remarkable," Fenian whispered, "that just as my life was meant to end, I found the person to make it worth living."

Allard shivered and Fenian's arms tightened around him.

"I don't know what to say," he breathed.

Fenian's voice in his mind was touched with amusement.

Don't say anything.

CHAPTER 17

ALLARD

They continued, riding well into the night until Fenian started to snore softly on Allard's shoulder, and he decided they had enough of a head start to take a short nap.

Allard didn't think he would be able to sleep when they laid under the trees, wrapped in the blanket. There was too much at stake. If they were caught, it would ruin all his plans.

That didn't stop him though, from accidentally falling into a deep slumber, tangled in Fenian's arms as though they were in the most secure and private place in the world.

Even the early morning light didn't rouse him. The only thing strong enough to drag Allard from his new lover's arms was the team of knights that had been sent after them.

"Rise and shine, Prince Allard," one of them said loudly.

Allard's eyes flew open, and he stared, confused, only for a moment at the sight of five knights above him, surrounding the spot where they lay.

Gasping, Allard shot up.

"Your highness," the familiar voice said. "If you do not resist, this will be easier for both of you."

Allard squinted at the knight, trying to place him through the helmet. He knew almost all of them, he often rode and trained with them. Normally, as their prince, he was treated with great respect and this sudden turn, where *he* was the villain, sent irritation flaring through him.

His gaze turned to Fenian. He was awake but still laying back on the blanket, propped on his elbows, looking unbothered.

He glanced at Allard.

We should probably run, he said.

How exactly do you propose we do that? We're surrounded.

Fenian pushed to his feet and dusted off his clothes with a heavy sigh.

"There's no use fighting, Allard, we're surrounded."

He looked at the knight who had spoken. Sir Clive, Allard finally realized. He usually headed the search parties. This was no different than usual for him, other than the fact that, as Allard knew the forest so well, he was usually riding next to the man.

"Sir Clive, you must know this isn't necessary. A search party to capture the crown prince is rather ridiculous, don't you think?"

Sir Clive pulled up his visor and peered at Allard regretfully.

"I'm sorry highness, I must follow my orders."

Allard pursed his lips.

"At the very least, I insist you leave my partner unshackled."

After a tense staring contest, Clive nodded.

He gestured to the others and both he and Fenian were taken by the arms and led back toward the path.

Their grip wasn't particularly strong, but forceful enough that Allard had to move when they pushed him.

They were led to separate horses.

Their eyes met as he hoisted himself atop the one offered to him, which, he noted, wasn't even his own.

He glanced over, finding that Blossom was already tied to one of the other horses, ready to be led back to the palace. It looked like she would have to be left behind.

There was no need for silent communication.

Without warning, Allard kicked the knight helping him straight into the chest, sending him stumbling back into the one behind him just as he kicked the horse forward.

Fenian was ready.

The moment Allard moved, he swung around, shocking the knight that held him with a strong shove. There was no use punching or hitting with the thick armor adorning them.

He made it one step, but that was all that was needed. They gripped each other's hands tightly and Fenian swung onto the back of the horse, arm landing around Allard's waist as they dove forward, but the knights blocked the path.

"Allard," Sir Clive said, voice grim. "Don't do this. Get off the horse or we'll have to use force."

"There's no way my father would order that," Allard said in disbelief.

"No, he wouldn't order us to hurt you," Clive agreed. "We'll aim for your friend."

Fenian laughed.

"Did he not even inform you of the details?" he demanded. "If you aim for me, you aim for him. Your prince will feel any physical pain you inflict upon me."

There was a tense moment of silence. Perhaps Sir Clive was weighing the validity of the claim.

"It's true," Allard added for good measure. "We are bound by magic... and for the record, Fenian is not my friend. He is my husband."

Fenian's arm tightened around Allard's midsection.

No one said anything. Perhaps they didn't know how to proceed after what he and Fenian had told them. When none of the knights moved to stop them, Allard turned the horse, heart ricocheting, and steered them the other way down the path.

Were they really going to let them go?

Apparently not, because Clive's voice rang through the air.

"Don't aim to kill."

Allard kicked, aware that Fenian was blocking him from any attacks but was himself, fully exposed. Their horse leaped forward, but too late.

Arrows flew past them. Behind them, there was the clink of metal armor as the knights mounted their steeds and a moment later, the thump of hooves was on their tail.

A sharp sting cut across the tip of Allard's ear and then faded just as fast. Behind him, Fenian cursed and shrank down against his back. He'd been grazed by an arrow.

Allard, his voice was loud and urgent in Allard's mind. *We must surrender. It's no use.*

"No!" he shouted.

He wasn't ready to give up. He never would be. He'd made his decision to leave the palace last night and he would rather take his chances running with Fenian than remain with the family that would not love him as he was.

The idea of accepting defeat so soon burned his chest like hot coals.

They had a head start. The others might fall behind.

He swung around to look and this time the pain that he suddenly felt did not fade a moment later. An arrow hit his arm, searing like fire, and sent him flying from the horse. He hit the hard, uneven ground next, scarcely missing being trampled. For a moment, his entire body was overwhelmed with so much pain that he couldn't breathe.

He wasn't aware of Fenian leaping from the horse, but suddenly he was at Allard's side, face pale in the dawning light of morning. His chest was heaving, eyes dark with concern.

"Allard," he whispered, hands hovering over him but never touching while he writhed in pain. Then, suddenly, he looked down the path from where they had come and then back at Allard, his gaze apologetic.

"I'm so sorry, Love," he whispered. "There's no time to be gentle."

And with that, he gripped Allard by the armpits and dragged him off the path, into the underbrush.

Sorry, sorry, he kept saying silently, every time pain shot through Allard's arm and back. Still, he did not stop until they were pressed up against the base of a large tree for support.

They weren't hiding though. They were still completely in the open. Allard bit his lip, hands clenching with the effort to remain silent.

He glanced down at his arm and saw the arrow pierced deep into his flesh. The world went fuzzy, and he squeezed his eyes shut, struggling to breathe and stay conscious.

Fenian's arm went around his shoulders, holding him tight and still, and then the knights arrived.

Allard watched in shock as they rode past.

Only the one closing the rear slowed, his gaze dropping to the path, tracing the obvious mark in the dirt where Allard's body had been pulled.

He followed the trail with his eyes, looking into the trees and then *directly* at them.

For a moment, Allard couldn't breathe. Then, to

his immense surprise, the knight carried on as though he didn't see them, following the others.

Still shocked, Allard stared at the now-empty path for a moment.

Finally, he thought to glance at Fenian who had his head bowed, eyes closed, a frown touching his brows.

"Are you responsible for what just happened?" he asked.

Fenian let out a relieved sigh.

"Are they all gone?"

Allard nodded.

"What did you do?"

"I made us blend into the shadows."

"That's more than just *blending in*."

Fenian shrugged.

"Elf magic is nothing more than using your own energy. Focusing it or dispersing it," he said. "I'm good at the big things; fire, light, explosions. Those who are good at the more subtle types of magic can actually make their bodies disappear. Me on the other hand, I can only camouflage us."

"One of them looked straight at us," Allard argued.

Fenian smirked.

"If he'd been an elf, he would have sensed us without even looking. Against beings as disconnected as humans though, I suppose we may as well have really been invisible."

Allard tried not to take offense to that.

"You do know I'm human, don't you? And that I took a damn *arrow* for you."

Fenian's smirk turned into a grimace.

"I know," he said.

He kissed Allard, stopping the argument *and* offering an apology with that one action. It did exactly as it was intended and calmed Allard's annoyance.

"That's one of the things I like about you," Fenian said softly when he pulled back.

"That I took an arrow for you?"

"That you don't hide things the way elves do. That you're honest and vibrantly alive. That you're human."

He smiled then.

"Now, about the arrow. You already made quite the impression when you chose to run away with me. There was no need to get shot as well."

Allard barely suppressed an eye roll.

With a steadying breath, he looked down at his arm again.

It hadn't pierced straight through the flesh of his arm, probably stopped by bone, judging by the way it felt.

When he didn't move at all, the pain wasn't as unbearable. It was a consistent burning though, and Allard didn't know what to do about that.

"You'll have to pull it out."

"I can't," Fenian argued and then, seeing Allard's expression, went on. "We have nothing to clean or bind the wound with. It's dangerous."

"I will not walk through the forest with an arrow protruding from my arm."

"What if the bleeding takes too long to stop?"

The tone of his voice drew Allard up short. Fenian was worried. Understandably so. Suddenly, Allard didn't quite know what to do.

"Tear my sleeve off," he said.

Fenian's gaze darkened, but he followed Allard's order, releasing him and gripping the fabric where it was already torn from the arrow, with one hard yank, it ripped apart, jarring Allard in the process.

He bit his lip, breathing through the pain of being jostled.

"Now the arrow," he grunted.

Fenian took the fabric, twisted it into a rope, and then held it to Allard's mouth.

"Bite."

Allard did and then, gritting his teeth, Fenian pulled.

He couldn't help the cry that tore from his lips.

For a moment, the world went dark from the pain. When it came back into focus, Fenian was holding him up, clamping a hand to his arm, looking pale.

"Oh good, you're staying awake," he breathed. "Give me that thing."

He took the rag and tied it tightly around Allard's bicep and then put his hands back over it for additional pressure.

"That's a lot of blood," Allard noted. "Is there supposed to be that much blood?"

Fenian shrugged.

"Not sure, I've never been shot before."

Anxiety filled him, along with slight lightheadedness. That didn't bode well. He forced himself to remain very still, closing his eyes against the sight.

For what felt like a long time, they sat like that, completely still, a worried look on Fenian's face whenever he chanced a glance at him until *finally*, the bleeding slowed.

"We wasted a lot of time. We should go."

"To Castero," Fenian said, more as a statement, like he fully expected Allard's nod and was not happy about it.

"We only need to make it past the border. Then we hitch a ride into the city. We will find a doctor there."

Fenian's lips twitched into a strange smile. He wouldn't look at Allard.

"Do you really think that will work?"

"It's less than a day's walk if that."

With a heavy sigh, Fenian released Allard's arm and pushed to his feet.

"Well then, let's not waste any time."

Pain seized him. He hadn't realized just how much he'd needed Fenian's steady strength to hold him still.

He tried to hide it though and struggled to his feet.

His back felt bruised and sore which didn't help but it was mostly the arm he was concerned about.

Finally standing, he nodded resolutely.

"To Casetro."

CHAPTER 18

FENIAN

*A*llard seemed to have forgotten that Fenian could feel his pain.

He was putting a mighty effort into hiding it each time he swung his arm too hard or stepped the wrong way. The sharp stinging was nearly enough to make Fenian sit down for a break and he knew Allard was experiencing a more constant version of what he was feeling.

Allard was strong-willed though, and stubborn and he'd put it in his head to go to Casetro so that they could be together. And so that was the direction they were headed, even though there was no longer a way that Fenian could allow that to happen.

A sharp cutting pain tore through his arm again

and he winced. Once it passed, he looked at Allard who had gone quite pale. He didn't seem to notice anything around him, not even the concern with which Fenian was watching him.

They couldn't walk the miles it would take to get across the border. They couldn't leave Allard bleeding like this.

The Elven Veil was closer. The medics there would be able to heal Allard within hours. Access to the healing pools alone would repair him… Although, Fenian would have to trade himself for that to happen and he didn't think Allard would take too kindly to that plan after all he had sacrificed for him.

The more Fenian thought of it, the more he was forced to acknowledge that Allard had given everything. And Fenian had taken everything.

But if they returned, like he was thinking they should, Fenian would have to give something all right. Their bond would be broken, Allard would be freed and Fenian's life would be on the line once more.

Was that a fair trade for a few hours of healing?

His stomach churned with the moral dilemma.

Considering that Allard hadn't yet suggested turning back for help, he could only assume Allard valued Fenian's life more than the discomfort of the wound currently ailing him.

He offered his arm, compelled to help in what little way he could.

Allard gripped it gratefully, leaning against him without any pretense. Without even denying how much he needed the support.

"Perhaps we should head back..." Fenian finally said.

Allard, face set in a grimace, eyes squeezed shut, didn't respond.

"Allard, did you hear me?"

"Of course, I heard you," he snapped. "I'm choosing not to respond to that ridiculous suggestion."

Frustration was Fenian's instant reaction to confrontation at the best of times. In this case, though, he managed to hold his tongue, mostly because it was Allard, and he'd grown to care about him so much in such a short time that it was frightening.

When another phantom pain shot through his shoulder though, he dug his heels in, forcing Allard to stop.

"You are not going to make it to Casetro," he informed him, forcing his voice to remain even.

Allard's gaze darkened.

"Yes, I will."

"You won't. You've lost too much blood already. Your arm is still bleeding now. If we head back to the Elven Veil, they will heal you."

"And sever our bond."

The pain in his eyes at that moment surpassed how they had looked even when he'd first been shot and Fenian's heart felt like it was being crushed.

"That doesn't change the fact that you will not be crossing that border on your own two feet."

Allard gripped his arm tighter, appealing to him with wide, worried eyes.

"So, carry me."

"Allard—"

"I can't give up Fenian. This is what I want. Me and you, standing together to face whatever we must."

It was sweet and moving and probably the thing Fenian had secretly wanted to hear his entire life; that someone cared enough for him that they would stand with him to the bitter end.

Only, it turned out that the passion directed at him did not go one way. He would not watch Allard die. Not for him.

Fenian was the criminal on death row. Allard was the virtuous prince who deserved the good life he had.

He had to fix this, to convince Allard to head back any way he could.

"Perhaps we can barter. They heal you in exchange for—"

"I won't return you to them, I already told you!" Allard snapped.

"That's not what I was going to say—"

"Then what—"

"You know I can feel it, right?" Fenian demanded. "Or did it escape your memory that we share our pain now, as well as our hearts?"

Allard paled.

"My arm—"

"Yes. And your leg and your back. You cannot hide it from me, Allard. And don't forget that if you die, I do as well."

"Oh. Is that the real reason you care so much? I know you're willing to do anything for your own life."

"Don't say that!" Fenian spat, furious. "I'm telling you I'm willing to trade mine, right now. Today. For you."

"Why bother?" Allard demanded, tears suddenly flooding his stormy gray eyes. "How do you honestly expect me to continue living after that?"

Silence rang between them, the air heavy.

Finally, Allard shook his head.

"It's impossible. I would never forgive myself. I would never move on. I—" Allard swallowed and cleared his throat, then continued more calmly. "Casetro is the only way. We will be there before nightfall. We must make it. There is no other choice."

Fenian swallowed the lump in his throat. His eyes burned with unshed tears. His heart felt physically heavy. He'd never been so invested in anyone in his entire life, had never hung on someone's every word, on the quiver in their voice and the reflections in their eyes.

He didn't *want* to turn himself in. He wanted the romantic getaway. He wanted to be with Allard, to find their future together, whatever that may be.

A deep spark of hope ignited in him, far stronger even than the fires he set.

For once, the life he fought for included the prospect of happiness and his entire being suddenly clung to that idea.

"If you get tired, promise me we will stop and rest."

Allard's eyes lit up. He inhaled a shuddering breath and leaned in, pressing a kiss to Fenian's lips as he smiled.

"Thank you," he breathed.

As Allard drew back, Fenian realized that something was wrong.

He wasn't as good with the subtle magics. His instincts for things like blending into the background, or noticing those that *did,* were limited to the basics.

While engrossed in conversation with the man that drew all his attention, it was no wonder that he didn't notice the beast until just as it leaped from the treetops.

Fenian's gaze flew up just as it dropped atop them. He caught sight of golden fur and sweeping brown wings and that was it before it hit them with the strength of a galloping horse.

Instantly winded, Fenian hit the ground hard, back smacking into it as the weight of the creature threw him down flat.

But it wasn't interested in him.

It wanted Allard, no doubt drawn by his blood.

It was atop Allard, and with the way they had fallen, both he and the *gryphon,* he realized, were pinning down Fenian's legs. Kicking furiously, fear gripping him, Fenian watched as the large beak tore mercilessly into Allard's shoulder.

Pain gripped him everywhere, a shout tore through his lips in unison with Allard before he suddenly fell silent. He was conscious or Fenian wouldn't be, but he was no longer fighting. His body was already limp and the world around Fenian was swiftly fading at the edges.

If he passed out now, if they both did, this was going to be one very happy creature. Fenian had fought too hard to become beast-meal.

Fenian's head fell back, but he fought the unconsciousness as it swiftly descended. He lifted his hands and with one last burst of energy, focused on his favorite trick.

Fire burst before him.

He didn't know if it hit Allard at first or the gryphon until the creature jumped back, a loud shriek piercing the forest, wings flapping as it lifted its heavy lion body into the air, smoke flowing from its singed fur.

"Allard," he gasped, but it was no use. Try as he might to remain conscious, afraid the beast wasn't done with them yet, Allard could no longer hold onto this world. *Hopefully, it is a temporary fade to darkness*, Fenian thought.

What a shame. He'd wanted to save Allard from a fate like this…

Fenian gasped awake, heart racing. He bolted upright, feeling as though he was being chased before his gaze fell on Allard, still sprawled on the forest floor, face down, golden hair a tangle atop his head, blood, and mud all over him.

They were awake! Another near-death dodged.

"Allard!" he scrambled to his husband, gripping him by the shoulders before gently turning him onto his back to see his face.

Pain stung through him as he moved Allard, but he ignored it as it was mild. Allard was possibly even numb from blood loss.

His pale gray eyes looked up, unseeing, barely open.

"Allard," Fenian said more gently. "Can you hear me?"

When he didn't answer, he tried again, going directly into Allard's mind, where he couldn't be so easily ignored.

My love, please tell me if you can hear me.

Yes.

Relief swamped him so fully Fenian could have collapsed from it.

Do everything you can to stay awake, he instructed, just as Allard's eyes began to droop again.

Desperately, Fenian held his face, brought his own so close that Allard finally looked at him. He pressed their foreheads together and whispered.

"Stay awake. For me."

For a moment, Allard didn't respond, and then, somehow, he seemed to focus, gaze growing sharper.

"Fenian," he whispered. "What happened?"

"You were attacked—*we* were. More animals will be drawn by the blood. There are more dangerous creatures in the Green Veil than we could count. We *must* move. Now."

With a momentous effort, Allard tried to sit. Fenian helped, noting the sweat breaking out over his skin and the way he gasped for breath by the time he was standing.

He swayed a little on his feet, gripping Fenian's shoulders like they were the only thing keeping him upright, which they probably were.

"All you must do is stay awake. I will get us there," Fenian promised. He hooked Allard's arm around his shoulders to take some of his weight and steered him through the trees.

They started with a slow pace, and it only grew slower as the exertion took its toll on Allard.

He didn't appear to still be bleeding from his wounds, but the amount of blood he'd lost to begin with was worrying. He looked exhausted.

Fenian suddenly woke up, sprawled on the soft earth, half atop Allard's prone body.

For a moment, staring up at the treetops, he

didn't know what had happened. And then he realized; Allard had passed out. They both had.

Cursing, he pushed up and turned to Allard, catching him blinking awake, moaning softly.

"One more time," he said. "Come on."

He hoisted Allard up.

The next time Fenian woke up, it was with his face buried in the moss at the base of a tree. Thankfully a small bit of air was reaching his nostrils or neither of them would have woken up at all.

"Fuck it all," he murmured and stood despite the way his body argued. "On my back this time."

Allard grumbled something, but Fenian could barely understand his quiet voice at this point.

Speak to me like this, he said silently. *It's less strenuous.*

I'm tired, Allard said.

I know. We're almost there.

The next time it happened, he felt the darkness swooping in and his legs giving out. At least he wasn't surprised to wake up sprawled on the forest floor that time. Next to him, Allard still seemed to be asleep, but he must have been at least a little conscious, or Fenian wouldn't be.

He reached out, desperation nearly overwhelming him, and grasped Allard's limp hand tightly, just to ground himself. They were cold though and his fear grew.

A sound reached him then. Like with the Gryphon, he sensed it a moment before it made its presence known.

He shot up and there, before him, a wolf froze, clearly surprised by his sudden movement.

It was large, like the gryphon, bigger than he could fight off physically on his own. It didn't look like it was immediately going to attack, it just watched them closely with sharp eyes, waiting just out of reach.

A chill traveling his spine, Fenian lifted his hand, sparking fire to the leaves scattering the earth at their feet.

The wolf's ears flickered, and it backed up a step before seeming to decide it wasn't worth it and turning tail.

Fenian waited until it was out of sight and then scoured the trees around them and above them, searching for more predators' watchful eyes.

Satisfied, he turned to Allard. His eyes were open now, staring blankly at the sky above.

"Are you okay?" he asked.

Allard didn't answer. Perhaps because he couldn't hear him. Perhaps because it was a pointless question. He was suffering.

Allard didn't deserve any of this. If Fenian had been better, Allard wouldn't be in this situation. He wouldn't be tied to the person who made his life unravel nearly to its end.

Well, all Fenian could do now, was make sure that he survived and beg for his forgiveness later.

An idea struck him, one that he would have thought narcissistic if not for the fact that over and over, Allard had shown how much he was willing to do for him.

Biting his lip, Fenian leaned over Allard, brushing the matted strands of golden hair from his forehead.

"If you don't force yourself to remain conscious, I will die with you," he whispered.

Finally, Allard's unfocused gaze sharpened.

He looked at Fenian and Fenian thought he might shout and cry at the same time.

"I'll carry you," he whispered. "Just stay awake."

Allard managed a weak nod.

It took maneuvering, but eventually, Fenian got Allard onto his back, hoisting him up.

Within a few minutes, Fenian was exhausted, his body protesting, but hopefully not enough that Allard felt it too. He didn't need any additional discomfort.

By the time they reached the main path, what should have taken an hour, had taken closer to three.

The Elven Veil wasn't far from there though. Fenian cut through the forest, focusing on each step forward, trying not to pay too much attention to how cold and clammy Allard's hands were around his shoulders or how much his heart ached. Probably through pure stubbornness, Allard stayed awake.

Fenian had finally found something meaningful enough to keep fighting for.

This person, the man he had chosen out of selfishness and desperation, seemed to love him. He would bet his entire being on it. He would endure beyond the point his body could handle, not for himself, but for Fenian. And Fenian... he would sacrifice himself for Allard.

And that was exactly what he intended to do.

Lost in thought, Fenian was caught by surprise when the elven guard materialized from the trees, surrounding them.

Their bows were drawn and suddenly, Seneca stepped from the trees, expression stern. Ready to punish Fenian, as always... and Fenian was so relieved, he collapsed to his knees.

Allard fell from his arms, onto the ground.

Pain lanced Fenian from the way he'd jostled his

husband. Ignoring the others, he bent over Allard as he moaned and shivered.

"I'm sorry," he whispered and pressed a kiss to his forehead. "It's all over now."

Allard blinked up at him.

"We heard of your escape, Fenian. The human king is not very pleased with us," Seneca said. "Coming here after running with the human prince was rather bold—"

"You can scold me later," Fenian interrupted. "He was shot by the human knights and injured again by a creature of the veil."

With a trembling breath, he pushed to his feet and faced Seneca.

"I am surrendering myself. Sever the bond. Execute me. It does not matter. Just heal him."

For once, emotion broke Seneca's cool exterior. Surprise.

He looked down at Prince Allard and then motioned to the guards.

"Take him to one of the pools. Now. Get the medic."

Fenian watched. Now that they were here, they couldn't move fast enough. Who knew how long Prince Allard had left? And then, they were lifting him, removing him as swiftly as they could between two of the guards. Suddenly, Fenian realized this might be his last chance to see Allard and anguish filled him.

And at that moment, perhaps because he knew he was safe now, Allard started to lose consciousness and Fenian followed.

I love you! He practically shouted to Allard, desperate for the last word before the world went completely dark once more.

CHAPTER 19

ALLARD

For a long time, Allard was sure he was in a nightmare. Moments flashed of extreme discomfort. Sometimes there was pain. For what felt like forever, he was being carried and jostled. Flashes of images accosted him; blinding streaks of sunlight, mud close to his face, deep blue, terrified eyes. That was the worst part.

Every time he saw Fenian, his lover was in anguish, dirt streaking his handsome face, long strands of his normally shining blue hair in tangles.

And then, at some point, there was peace.

Allard felt nothing but the occasional sensation that he was floating in the clouds. There were soft blue lights around him when he opened his eyes and lovely embroidered fabrics and beautiful, unfamiliar faces. During one of these brief moments of consciousness, he realized that the people he saw were elves.

Something told him that was a bad thing, but for the life of him, Allard couldn't remember why.

Eventually, when Allard woke up properly, he was completely alone in a familiar room filled with natural wood carvings and intricate tapestries.

There was a chill in the air, goosebumps on his skin despite the thin blanket draped over him, and he was completely alone.

Ah, yes. The Elven Veil. One of the loneliest places that Allard had ever visited.

He tried to move, to sit up or even lift his arm, but his hand only rose an inch. His body was too exhausted to do more than that.

Suddenly, someone was next to him, offering to help.

"Glad to see that you are awake, Prince."

He was lifted slightly, a pillow wedged under his head to offer more of a horizontal position, and then a glass of water was pressed to his lips.

Allard gratefully gulped the cold, refreshing liquid before collapsing back against the pillows and looking up at the unfamiliar elf.

He didn't recognize her and was quite sure he would recall such vibrant pink eyes and hair. She smiled at him kindly.

"I am your medic, Leona," she explained. "My colleagues and I are responsible for healing your wounds. You were lucky to have made it here when you did."

Frowning, Allard forced his voice out, but still, it came out scratchy and barely audible.

"What happened?"

"You were hit by an arrow and then attacked by a creature of the Green Veil, drawn by the blood."

Allard stared.

He remembered the arrow now. His foolish knights shouldn't have fired them, at all. Clearly, someone in the chain of command hadn't believed that Allard and Fenian were bound in that way and Allard would bet that it had been his father. If the arrow had landed where it had been intended, in Fenian's back, they could both be dead right now.

The creature that Leona mentioned though, Allard had no recollection of. He also didn't remember how he happened to arrive here, but even with a foggy brain, he drew the obvious conclusion.

"Fenian brought me here," he whispered.

She nodded.

"Where is he?"

"I believe that is for the council to discuss with you."

Distressed, Allard tried once more to sit but she pushed him gently back down.

"The bond," he gasped, as the room began to spin.

"You are still recovering from the blood loss. You must rest," she insisted.

"The bond is still intact."

Allard looked toward the door, surprised by Seneca's sudden arrival.

"Fenian," he managed to say.

"He's being held right now."

"The bond—"

"It has not been severed. Can't you feel it?"

Seneca came forward, dismissing Leona who quickly exited to give them privacy.

"Shut your eyes," Seneca instructed. "Try to feel Fenian's presence."

Allard did as he was told. Shutting his eyes, he was forced to breathe through the panic until it ebbed enough that he could try to sense his husband. He'd never tried it before, so it came as a shock when he realized that Fenian was right there. A hint of fleeting emotions that were not his own. Resentment. Worry. Sadness.

Then, mind finally clear enough, he realized that

whether Fenian was with him or not, as long as the bond was intact, they could still converse.

Fenian, he whispered.

There was a moment's silence and then, Fenian's relieved voice.

You're properly awake. I could honestly cry.

Don't do that.

Are you okay? How do you feel?

Assessing himself, Allard blinked his eyes open and found Seneca watching him closely.

"Satisfied?" the elf asked.

Allard nodded.

"How did I get here?"

"Fenian carried you. He turned himself in, in exchange for your life."

Allard swallowed.

"What is next?"

"That is still to be decided," Seneca said. "Your father insists on the bond being broken."

"And Fenian? Will he be executed if that happens?"

Seneca didn't answer for a long moment.

"I cannot promise anything. The decision is not mine alone."

Allard. Are you there? Can you hear me?

I can hear you, he answered.

Then why won't you answer me? Fenian demanded.

Because I'm angry with you. You promised *me we wouldn't come back here.*

A long silence rang between them and then Fenian laughed.

If you're well enough to be angry with me, I will take it as an indication of your good health.

"Are you able to use inner speak?" Seneca suddenly asked, brows raised.

Surprised, Allard shrugged.

"With Fenian, yes."

"That's very interesting. For a human to obtain a specifically elven trait is unheard of."

"Is it?" Allard frowned. "I believe we just share everything now. Even this."

A soft smile touched Seneca's lips.

"That is probably true. I suppose I wouldn't know. I've never known an elf who wed a human, even in all these years."

"How old are you?" Allard asked, curiosity eating at him.

"Older than a human could live," Seneca said. "When last I counted, my age was nearing two hundred years."

Shocked, Allard stared at his relatively youthful face. Like many of the elves, it was hard to place an age on him. He appeared young enough, perhaps middle-aged, yet his maturity made him seem older.

"In all this time, you never wanted to bond with someone?" he asked.

Seneca smiled again, a soft, melancholic smile that didn't quite reach his eyes.

"I did bond with someone," he finally admitted, "a long time ago."

Allard shook his head, trying to remember being introduced to a partner but aside from the council and guards, he'd never seen Seneca with anyone.

"I'm sorry, I must have forgotten. I don't recall anyone."

"You wouldn't," Seneca said. "He passed on shortly after our bond, which was severed just before he left our realm."

Shocked, Allard stared at Seneca. He remembered all the things Seneca had said would happen if his bond was severed; that he would be incomplete, unable to love again, a shadow of his former self. He swallowed back the sudden lump in his throat.

"Why?"

"Because he could not be healed, and I was already on the council... It was for the greater good to remain here without him."

Allard stared at him for a long moment.

"And that's what you think I should do now? Sever our bond and carry on in my position. For the greater good."

For a moment, Seneca didn't answer. His gaze landed on the window and then, to Allard's shock, he shook his head.

"No," he whispered. "It is not what I think you should do. Living without your bonded partner is a fate worse than death. It is excruciating and... it isn't fair to do that to anyone."

Tears abruptly stung Allard's eyes.

He reached out without thinking and gripped Seneca's arm.

"I'm sorry," he whispered. "But please. Can't you stop this? Can't you just let us go?"

"I am not the only person who has a right to decide. The council will vote and then, of course, there is the human king. Your parents are currently on the way here to discuss the matter. That said... you have my support."

"What about me?" Allard asked. "Doesn't my choice mean anything?"

"That is a very strong argument, indeed."

He reached down and patted Allard's hand.

"I will let you rest," he said and then paused, expression thoughtful. "Perhaps later I can give you that tour I owe you. You never did see much of the Elven Veil."

Allard wasn't interested in a tour. Truth be told, he didn't care much for the elves anymore. All he wanted to do was take Fenian away from this place and never look back.

CHAPTER 20

ALLARD

*D*espite Allard's lack of interest in the tour, Seneca still showed up to take him on one.

The elves were miraculous healers and after a long nap, and a hearty meal, Allard didn't even have an excuse not to go.

"I'll just clean myself up," he told the elf.

Seneca nodded and took a seat next to the bookshelf, selecting a title to read while he waited.

When Allard stood, his body creaked a little from not being used, but other than that, he wasn't in the worst shape. His body was still stiff, but in a way that he thought moving might fix, so he slipped into the soft, elven slippers that had been left by his bed and went to the washroom.

The first thing Allard did was go to the mirror and look at himself. The long white robe he wore was soft but heavy. It hung to his ankles and was tied securely all along one side so that no skin peeked through.

Carefully, he peeled the fabric off his shoulders, letting it fall to his elbows.

Where the arrow had pierced, there was now a pale, shiny scar that looked fresh, but clean, like it wouldn't be visible for long. The skin on his shoulder though remained red and uneven. When he ran his fingers over the beaded flesh, it was smooth and hard. He could see what looked like puncture wounds from claws perhaps, and the largest part of the scar, where it looked like his flesh had been torn apart.

The creature had taken a good chunk out of him or had tried at least. If not for Fenian...

Hey Fenian, what exactly attacked me?

A gryphon. It dropped atop you from the trees. If not for my handy fire...

Allard swallowed, considering the wound with new appreciation.

Now that he looked again, he could see that the marks were from talons and a beak.

Shuddering, Allard pushed the thought away.

You saved us.

It was the least I could do, considering I was the reason you were in that position, to begin with.

Allard bit his lip. He wanted to argue, but not now.

Seneca is waiting for me. He wants to give me a tour of the Elven Veil.

Delightful, Fenian said dryly.

Mmhm. Any sights that I simply cannot miss?

Fenian seemed to consider before speaking.

I hear the prison is a sight to behold. Especially the sole prisoner currently behind bars.

Allard held back a laugh.

Oh, is that so? he asked in return. *What's so special about him?*

Just the company he keeps, I wager, Fenian said.

Allard could hear the smile in his voice, but his words still made him somehow sad.

I beg to differ, he said softly.

For a moment, Fenian didn't reply.

Don't leave your tour guide waiting.

Allard sighed. He wanted to refuse but he couldn't pretend he wasn't able to go on a stroll. Seneca would see straight through him.

He did look tired though and his hair was in

disarray, so he took time with the washbasin and brushes provided to clean himself up.

When he emerged, he felt a little bit more like himself.

"My clothes?" he asked.

"I apologize, but we disposed of them," Seneca said. "They didn't appear salvageable."

Torn and dirty, Allard assumed. Although he wasn't looking forward to seeing his father, he hoped that he would at least arrive with some human clothes for him. In the meantime, the elven wear would have to do.

"Is this acceptable to go outside in?" he asked, gesturing to the long white robe.

Seneca nodded.

"Of course."

He held the door open and gestured for Allard to pass through.

Allard followed Seneca through the streets of the Elven Veil. Like before, he was amazed by the peaceful quality of the very air.

If people yelled here, he wagered it was directly into each other's minds. It did not seem like elves ever lost their composure.

Yet Fenian was so passionate. Allard wondered how had he survived so many years here?

This time, instead of moving away from the city center, Seneca directed him toward it.

Once again, Allard faced the giant pit in awe.

Staircases had been carved directly into the cliffs on all sides and they took one down while Seneca explained about the production of the chasm over a thousand years before in hopes of expanding without further disruption to the rest of the forest.

Allard was beyond impressed.

So little light reached into the depths that their lights were spelled across all surfaces. Even the air was overcome by glowing moths and other bugs fluttered and buzzed throughout until the entire pit glowed brightly.

"I've never seen bugs like these," he said.

"It's a spell," Seneca explained. "Any insects with wings that fly below a certain point develop a glow. Over the years, many ways of adding natural light sources were attempted. This was one of the more successful spells. Since the chasm is so big, it requires a team of at least fifty mages to replenish it every several years."

"Wow," Allard breathed.

The human dungeons were downright laughable compared to this. Then again, they weren't exactly meant to be comfortable.

"You must have found the human town incredibly basic," he laughed.

Seneca didn't answer, apparently concentrating on his steps as they continued to descend.

When they finally reached the bottom, he paused and looked at Allard closely.

"Did that take too much out of you?" he asked. "We can rest before continuing."

Allard shook his head.

He was tired, but he didn't want to rest. Now that they were here, he was eager to see more.

Taking him at his word, Seneca turned and continued to lead him through the streets.

"Directly ahead of us, you will see the university."

Allard followed Seneca in awe as he gave him a quick tour through the grounds, including the enchanted gardens, the nature of which, Allard had never imagined before.

Seneca, face a constant calm mask, made Allard attempt to school his excitement, even though the trees danced to the music that a violinist played for them from a stand.

I think I saw a nymph! he practically shouted to Fenian.

Fenian's warm laugh met his ears.

Ah, the university gardens, I take it. I used to love sitting there, listening to the flute players.

Allard could imagine Fenian there, sitting on one of the benches, feeling the soft breeze, letting the trees sweep their low hanging branches through his midnight hair.

Did you come here a lot?

Nearly every day, Fenian confirmed. *I was raised nearby.*

His interest peaked, Allard followed Seneca who continued to tell him about the design of the gardens, why it was placed just there so that the creak could flow into the small lake.

Sure enough, a small, gentle waterfall cascaded over the cliffside, slapping the lake with the mesmerizing chatter of water hitting water.

"It's beautiful here."

Seneca nodded.

"The university grounds are certainly a point of pride for us. This way."

He gestured to one of the paths, leading Allard on.

"Fenian said he was raised near here," Allard said, eying Seneca.

The elf didn't show any signs of surprise. Perhaps he expected Fenian to be an unseen companion on this tour.

"He did live near here. Just ahead."

Seneca paused when they reached a building.

It didn't appear to be a home, just a rather non-descript building by elf standards. In fact, it looked more like a school.

"I used to tutor Fenian here."

"I thought you said he lived here."

"He did. This is the home for orphans."

"Oh."

Fenian had mentioned not having a family, yet he hadn't imagined him being raised in an orphanage.

"He really lived here?"

"Him and one other child, Sabina."

Sabina. Allard knew that name. The victim of Fenian's fatal fire.

"They were raised together?" Allard asked uneasily. Fenian hadn't mentioned that part. Although, it must have been hard enough to talk about. At the time, if he had known Allard had been listening, he might not have shared anything at all.

"It is rare for elves to be without their parents. Due to the same accident, Fenian and Sabina were orphaned together and raised here."

Allard's heart constricted.

"Who watched over them?"

Seneca tilted his head, thoughtfully.

"They were old enough to care for themselves for the most part," he said. "They had tutors and sched-uled activities to teach them to be part of society in the way their parents would have. They attended community events, and in the meantime, they were checked on and their needs met."

Allard found that whole system too confusing to follow for a moment.

"So... they were left to their own devices after losing their parents? Only, with teachers coming for classes and their food being delivered?"

Allard hoped with a sinking feeling, that he was wrong, but that was certainly how it sounded.

Alas, Seneca nodded.

"Perhaps it is hard to fathom for a human, but by our standards, they were well cared for... I should know. I was here every day to check on them. As was Yana and countless others in various roles."

Allard bit his tongue.

Being checked on by any number of people was not the same as having someone there for comfort, peace of mind, to hug, or to talk to. The security of even knowing that you weren't alone, that you didn't need to fend for yourself was more important to a child than anything.

Allard knew firsthand. Growing up in a large castle had its drawbacks and his parents had always been busy. Still, he'd often found himself slinking through the shadowy corridors past watching knights to their room in the middle of the night.

At times when they weren't around, sometimes he'd had tantrums and been so frustrated that he didn't know how to act, Sten would sit next to him, requiring nothing and offering only his steady presence until Allard calmed down again.

Knowing that you weren't alone, that you had support was, in his humble opinion, the key to finding confidence within oneself as an adult.

Suddenly the door flew open, and a small child tumbled from within, stumbling to a stop as his large, round eyes caught sight of Allard and Seneca standing on the path.

For a moment, Allard was blown away by the lovely silver of his eyes and hair and then he noticed the tremble in the small child's chin and the glossy sheen to his gaze.

"Shouldn't you be in class?" Seneca asked.

The child sniffled up at him but didn't answer. Instead, his wide gaze fixed on Allard.

"You look different," he said.

Allard smiled and knelt, putting himself closer to the boy's level.

"I look different because I am not an elf. I'm human."

Slowly, he came forward, watching Allard curiously. His gaze fell to the white robe, and he reached out, touching it.

"Are you sick?" he asked.

The worry in his tone made Allard's heart ache for him. He was so small, surely no more than three or four, but he knew illness. Being that he was an orphan, Allard could guess why.

"I'm all better now," he reassured. For a moment, the child didn't seem convinced, and then, he smiled, eyes brightening.

"That's good."

"What's your name?" Allard asked.

Before he could answer, the door flew open again and a female elf flew through.

She stopped dead when she saw them and sighed.

"Liamar," she scolded. "What are you doing out here?"

She came forward, nodding to both Allard and Seneca while the child, Liamar, shifted subtly so that Allard was half-blocking him from her.

"I want to play."

"You can't go play during lessons. I only left him for a minute," she explained to Seneca.

He smiled.

"Don't worry, Sabina, I know they never want to stay put at his age."

A strange feeling ran down Allard's spine like a drip of cold water.

Sabina.

"I should know," she said with a soft smile.

"Are you enjoying your new duty?" Seneca asked. She nodded.

"It's comfortable to be back here," she said. "I'm happy to give back."

Allard had to say something, he had to know. The words slipped from his mouth without thought.

"Are you fully healed now?" he asked. "From the burns?"

She glanced at him and then slowly nodded.

"Yes," she said. "I'm mostly myself again."

Suddenly, the world seemed to close in around him. Blood rushed through his ears. His heart started to race.

Her gaze flew to Seneca.

"I apologize," he said. "This is Prince Allard, of the humans... He is Fenian's bonded husband."

The way he said it, paired with the subtle look he gave her, seemed to convey everything left unsaid. Her eyes widened slightly, and she looked at Allard again with great curiosity.

"How is Fenian?" she asked.

A touch of concern entered her voice and Allard's confusion grew. He didn't know what to make of any of this.

"He's in a cell," he said. "Waiting to be executed. For ending *your* life."

She paled but did not so much as twitch.

Her gaze went to Seneca again and he stepped forward, taking Liamar by the shoulders and steering him toward Sabina.

"Back to class," he said. "Both of you."

Sabina placed a hand on Liamar's shoulder, leading him back inside, but she paused, gaze lingering on Allard as though she wanted to say something.

Finally, she seemed to think better of it and turned her back to them, silently entering the orphanage.

A hand touched Allard's back and he spun around, slapping it away.

"What is the meaning of this?" he demanded.

"Let us talk somewhere more private."

"No," Allard snapped. "I'm not going anywhere with you until I get an explanation."

Seneca raised a brow.

"I suppose I should have expected such a passionate reaction from someone of your kind."

Allard laughed bitterly.

"Oh please, do not pretend that you elves are so much better. Not now that I know you callously execute those who have done *nothing* wrong."

For once, more than a flicker of emotion showed on Seneca's face.

He gritted his jaw, nostril's flared and for a moment, Allard thought he was going to get an earful. Then Seneca turned his face away, took a deep breath, and with a slow exhale, his composure returned.

Unfortunately, Allard didn't know that trick and he was absolutely *livid*.

"She's alive. She's *working*. She's completely fine! What is Fenian doing in that cell? Why would you do this?"

His shouts echoed back to him. In the cavernous depths of the city center, all big sounds did. Perhaps that was why it was so quiet down there.

Allard didn't care though. All he could think about was the fact that Fenian had nearly lost his life over something that hadn't happened. That he had been so desperate to live that he had forced the bond with Allard. That he was being persecuted even now, while Sabina carried on with her regular life.

"What do you believe happened?" Seneca asked.

Allard blinked and tried to pull his jumbled thoughts and emotions together.

"He set a fire—"

"Yes, to commit a robbery. After countless others."

Allard swallowed and went on.

"He set a fire. He didn't know Sabina was inside.

She got hurt but *didn't* die."

"Correct."

Allard stared at Seneca.

"Do you really not think this is wrong?" he asked, genuinely confused. "Surely elves have *hearts* and *morals*. You're punishing an innocent person."

"I argued it at first," Seneca confessed, "until I saw the truth. From a young age, Fenian carried out one crime after another. Sabina was his first victim, but if we'd allowed him to carry on, she would not have been his last. I believed my comrades were right. Even the night he bound himself to you, he started a fire in the explosives warehouse without even knowing if anyone was nearby. There could have easily been victims to his selfish, careless act."

"But there *weren't.*"

Seneca nodded.

"That is precisely my issue, Prince Allard. Why do you think I brought you here?"

Allard shook his head, at a loss.

"I told you this morning. I am not the only person who decides. This time, instead of running, make an appeal with the council."

He reached out, placed a hand on Allard's shoulder, and squeezed.

"Don't take no for an answer."

CHAPTER 21

FENIAN

Fenian sat on the bed in his cell, staring out at the trees pensively.

He couldn't say that he was happy to be back here, but for the fact that Allard was okay. He was alive, he was safe... he was currently strolling through the setting of Fenian's most familiar memories.

Nostalgia settled over him.

He didn't often think of his childhood. He tried not to, anyway, especially since Sabina's untimely end.

Guilt stirred in him.

Their fathers had worked together in the fishery. Of course, Fenian had been too young to know that until after their boat sank, drowning them both, and taking their partner's lives with them.

He and Sabina had always gotten along the way children did. Occasionally they argued, but Sabina was older and more level-headed and often found a way to make amends. Fenian wasn't as good at that part. He wasn't good at apologizing.

He wasn't good at a lot of things.

He'd spent so much time skipping the classes and civic duties that were bestowed upon orphans at a young age, turning instead to vandalism and crime.

It was strange to think of Allard being there. To imagine him walking the university grounds and the path to the orphanage was surreal. It was like his old world and new one were mingling when they shouldn't have ever crossed paths.

For some reason, he wished he could keep Allard away from all that. He didn't want him to see those parts of him; the parts that he was most embarrassed by.

How is your tour going? he asked, unable to bear the long silence that had dragged on between them.

After a moment, Allard answered, the tone of his voice unreadable.

I think... I hate this place.

Laughter burst from Fenian's lips.

Across the path, he could see the guard turn to look at him curiously.

Fenian shrugged and laid back in bed, still smiling. Allard's distaste for whatever he saw down there was oddly mollifying.

Are you going to miss me? he asked.

Immediately, he felt bad. He didn't know why he'd suddenly switched to such an unhappy topic, but now that it was out, he held his breath, waiting for Allard's answer.

No. Allard said sharply and Fenian's heart rate spiked anxiously, even though he knew it wasn't true.

So, you're still mad at me for all of this then? he asked.

I'm not mad at you, Allard said softly. *I'm just not planning on leaving without you.*

Fenian smiled softly.

That was the prince he knew. There was so much that Fenian didn't know about Allard. They'd had so little time together. But he did know that he was the type who would never give up, no matter what happened.

Laying on his narrow bed, he realized that they'd never even shared one.

For the entirety of their relationship, they'd been running and hiding and in discomfort. Cold, hard bars, muddy forest earth, damp, rough dungeons… it really was a wonder that Allard had thought it worthwhile. He deserved a soft bed, warm, clean blankets, and Fenian's arms around him all night.

That was never going to happen though. He couldn't imagine that they would manage another hasty getaway and the elven council would accept no bargaining.

He thought of Allard, so sweet, so full of love and desperate to share it, and had to swallow back the bile in his throat.

He wouldn't be the same after the bond was severed, but at least Fenian wouldn't have to know how bad it was for him.

He would no longer be on this earth and for that, he was almost grateful.

Being apart physically was hard enough. Once the bond between their souls was cut apart, he didn't think he would be able to bear it.

How selfish, he thought. *Accepting my end so that I don't have to feel it while Allard is left to deal with that pain alone...*

His fists gripped the blankets tightly as doubt filled him, but too late because just then, a shadow fell over him.

Two guards stood on the other side of the bars,

one holding the key to his cell, the other holding handcuffs to put him in.

They're here to take me, Fenian told Allard. He could hear the panic in his voice, but Allard's immediate response was comforting.

It's okay Fenian. Go with them. They're bringing you to me.

Surprised, Fenian stood as they entered.

"Are these really necessary?" he asked, nodding to the handcuffs. "I turned myself in. It's not very likely I'm going to run, is it?"

Neither of them responded.

Sighing, Fenian offered his hands and didn't argue when he was cuffed, taken by both arms, and led from the cell.

"Where are you taking me?" he asked. Not because he didn't trust that Allard *thought* they were bringing Fenian to him, but because he didn't trust his brethren.

He'd learned that his people were sneaky by nature, always believing their reasons were just.

After a long pause, one of them answered.

"To the council."

Sure enough, poor Allard was being misled. He didn't understand elves quite as well as Fenian did.

Fenian had been left alone while Allard healed, most likely because the bond could not be severed while they were both unconscious. Now that Allard was healed though, it was time to officially close this chapter, Fenian assumed.

They headed toward the council's meeting area, set away from society, on the edge of the Elven Veil. It was a simple space, with cleared trees and an area to sit. Fenian had always assumed that was to keep trouble far from the rest of the elves and to easily contain any issues that arose.

It also meant there was less distance to the wilderness if one were to run, of course, and it was probably the reason he'd found a place to consummate the bond with Allard.

He clung to that memory as he entered the space, eager to hold onto a moment that held so much meaning to him, and then stopped in his tracks at the sight that met him.

Allard was indeed there, along with the council and the human king and queen. This time, a table and chairs had been set on the platform, presumably to make the humans more comfortable, but Fenian didn't care about any of it. Allard was all he could see.

Emotion overcame him as he shook the guards off and strode into the clearing.

Allard saw him at once and stood, marching toward him.

As they reached each other, Fenian lifted his cuffed hands, throwing his arms around Allard's shoulders and pulling him into a tight embrace that was returned with equal amounts of desperation and relief.

For a moment, they stood like that, breathing each other in and it became more and more apparent how much Fenian had needed this. The last time he'd seen Allard, he'd been hanging on to life by a thread. He'd watched him be carried away and he hadn't been able to breathe easy since. But he was here now.

"You're okay," he breathed.

Allard chuckled.

"Of course. I told you I was."

He pulled back just enough to press a kiss to Fenian's lips and Fenian held on tighter, embarrassed as tears suddenly burned his eyes.

Allard abruptly broke away and glanced back at the others. Of course. His parents didn't approve. No one did, in fact, and they were sitting there, waiting for them. Fenian thought he might puke from the nerves.

"Come on," Allard said.

Wait? Fenian asked.

Allard looked at him and his gaze softened. He positioned himself, blocking Fenian from view while he tried desperately to get his emotions in check. The damn tears were proving hard to stop though, especially when Allard stroked his hair comfortingly.

Everything is going to be okay, he said, *we're just going to talk.*

Somehow, that actually *was* a comfort. Still, Fenian was half sure that their bond was about to be broken and he wasn't ready to face that fact.

I promise, Allard said, looking intently into his eyes. *I asked them to come to hear my appeal.*

Fenian's eyes widened, and a sad smile touched his lips.

It was remarkably sweet that Allard thought they would listen to him. The elven council never listened, not even to their own kind. Fenian had learned that the hard way. He had allowed himself to hope before and he wasn't planning on doing it again, but Allard appeared so serious, so confident, despite the parlor of his skin and the dark circles under his eyes. He was still recovering from his wounds, but that wasn't stopping him.

Fenian swallowed and somehow managed to get his emotions in check. At his nod, Allard shot him a small smile and took him by the hand, leading him back to the group.

They were silent, all the council watched them approach with their usual unreadable masks. Allard's mother stared. Her wide gray eyes, so much like her son's bounced between them and their clasped hands. His father, however, glared at the trees beyond.

Fenian wasn't surprised. After all, the only other time he'd seen the king, he'd punched Fenian across the face.

Allard pulled him onto the seat next to him without releasing his hand and then cleared his throat, ready to start the meeting.

"Let us begin," he said.

Fenian couldn't help smiling, despite himself. Allard truly had no regard for the age and position of the elven council or even his own father. He meant business, and Fenian adored that brazen, confident streak he had.

"There is nothing to discuss," his father said, straightening and leveling his son with a look. "We have already made our decision."

Allard glanced at the council members and to Fenian's surprise, Seneca backed him.

"*We* have not yet made our decision," he said tersely. "I told you before and I shall repeat it now. We will not be bullied into doing what we disagree with."

"You would rather a war?" the king demanded, cheeks turning red.

Surprised, Fenian's gaze shot to the council members. There was no way that they would start a war over *him*.

"True, we will not be forced to agree with you, but in this case, I agree, we will do as the king says and carry on with our original plan for Fenian. This is incontestable" Kial said, leveling a gaze at Seneca. "I'm surprised at you, continuing to stir trouble."

"Do not speak to me like that," Seneca warned. "I have good reason for holding my ground."

"Seneca is correct," Yana interjected, glancing at Allard. "Our decision did not include an innocent life when we first made it."

"Yes," Allard said. "It is *my* life, and I would like to address it. That is why I called you all here today."

He turned to his parents; gaze hard when it landed on the king.

"Father," he said. "Let me make one thing completely clear to you. If the bond is severed and Fenian dies, I will still follow him."

Fenian's heart dropped.

Allard's mother gasped.

What are you saying? he demanded but Allard didn't answer him. His gaze remained unwaveringly on his fathers.

"You don't mean that."

"I do," he said at once and Fenian could hear the truth in his voice. "I have it on very good authority that once a bond is broken, life is no longer worth living."

A long silence rang in the air.

"Besides," Allard went on. "Even if removing the bond didn't affect me at all, it's not what I want. I want to be with Fenian."

He glanced over, meeting Fenian's wide stare.

"I know you don't approve of this type of love between two men, but I would rather lose you than remain with a family that doesn't accept me for who I truly am."

"But Allard," his mother suddenly said, her voice soft and worried, eyes rimmed with tears. "You never showed interest in men before. He *tricked* you."

Allard shook his head and then spoke, his voice quavering.

"I *was* interested in men before. I was too scared to be honest with you. I knew you wouldn't approve."

He swallowed and then turned his attention to the elven council, voice hardening when he spoke.

"As for the other issue. I'm quite certain that Fenian wouldn't have felt pressured into forcing a bond with me if not for the fact that he was about to be executed for something that he *didn't even do.*"

The words didn't process. Not even when Allard looked him straight in the eyes and squeezed his hand under the table.

Fenian looked at the other elves, confused by the shame flickering over their faces.

"We had our reasons for doing what we did," Yana said gently to him. "Between the group of us, we rarely make choices that I regret. Now though, I wonder if it was too extreme."

"It wasn't," Kial snapped. "We had good reason to remove him from elven society."

Everyone was looking at Fenian, but he couldn't think straight.

He shook his head.

"What are you saying?"

"A little over an hour ago, I met the person whose death you were being punished for," Allard said. "Sabina is still alive."

Fenian could see the anger in his eyes. He knew Allard was telling the truth, but he couldn't accept it.

"No. She was in the building. I didn't mean to but—"

"She was hurt," Allard agreed, "but that was it. She's fully healed and carrying on with her life as though nothing happened."

Sabina wouldn't agree to that. Fenian knew she wouldn't. Not unless she was given strict instructions to keep away from him.

He looked at the council members as his shock morphed to something else. An incredulous laugh left him.

"Oh, I see. It all makes sense now." He met Yana's gaze. "I suppose I am *Dawna*. I was naive enough to believe that the council would never lie and betray their own kind to such a degree. I didn't even question it when you told me she perished... For months, I've lived with the guilt of accidentally killing the only person who was close to being my family."

For a minute, they remained silent. Fenian knew they were discussing the matter between them, silently so no one else could interfere. Finally, Yana spoke.

"The execution is off," she said.

Fenian would have been relieved if he was not so angry.

"And the bond?" Allard demanded. "What of that?"

"I'm sorry son," the king piped in, "but this is between *him* and the elves. It has nothing to do with you anymore. I will not change my mind."

Allard's lips twisted with distaste.

"I suppose you don't believe my threat," he said. "I

can't say I'm surprised. After all, you clearly ordered the knights to attack Fenian, despite being told that I would get hurt too. I nearly died because of you."

The king paled.

"It's true," Seneca said. "It was very a very foolish choice shooting at them. Your son was lucky enough to have Fenian to carry him here on his back. He was willing to sacrifice himself for Prince Allard's safety."

"Are you trying to convince me that this elf is worthy?" he demanded. "He's a criminal!"

Allard stood.

"Father, Mother, and council members... I believe that Fenian has served enough time for the crimes he *actually* committed. I will now be leaving this place with my husband at my side."

Yana, speaking for the council, rose and smiled.

"I think under these circumstances, you are correct. We will not stop you. Fenian, you are free."

Fenian couldn't believe what he was hearing. He stood, feeling almost light-headed.

"Dear," Allard's mother said, rising, her voice small. "I don't mind this arrangement if it means keeping you close."

She looked at Fenian and for the first time, offered him a smile.

"I want my son to be happy and healthy and I

have never seen him fight for something as hard as he's fighting for you."

Moved, Fenian almost wanted to hug the woman.

Allard didn't have the same reservations because he went and pulled her into a tight embrace.

"Thank you, Mother," he whispered.

When he pulled back, he looked down at his father, still seated in his chair scowling.

"And you, Father?" he asked tentatively. "Please. Would you give Fenian and I a chance?"

He was a stubborn man, understandably used to getting his way. Perhaps that was why he was so slow to respond.

"It does not appear as though I have a choice," he finally said.

Allard clearly took that as a yes, because he grinned and hugged his father's shoulders.

"I don't like this," he said gruffly and then fixed a piercing gaze on Fenian. "You will have to work hard to prove yourself and make amends for forcing this situation in the first place."

"Of course," Fenian agreed at once, heart soaring. "I'll do anything to be with Allard."

That statement seemed to surprise King Jareth, and for the first time, the anger started to ebb from his face.

Allard met his gaze. A grin lifted his expression,

happiness practically pouring out of him and Fenian felt the same, as though he might float away.

He had gone through so many intense emotions in such a short space of time that it was dizzying. Fear, excitement, relief, anger, but now *happiness* pushed the rest of them away.

He had never known what being safe and whole, truly felt like. As Allard pulled him into a warm embrace, he had a feeling he was soon to find out.

CHAPTER 22

ALLARD

*A*llard still couldn't believe they had gotten away with all this.

The fact that his demands had been met so fully was both gratifying and heartwarming. It was nice to know that his parents cared about him enough to set their differences aside.

His harsh ultimatum that day in front of his parents and the elven council had not been empty threats. Allard had truly meant what he'd said. After learning the injustice that Fenian had been put through, and hearing from Seneca how hard life was without his husband, he would have refused point-blank to allow anything but *this*.

"Ready?" Sten asked.

Allard took one last look at himself in the mirror. He was in a traditional wedding suit, one that was fit for a prince. The white fabric gleamed, accentuated by golden threading and embroidered designs.

Apparently, Fenian's suit matched Allard's, but with slight differences. He hadn't seen it yet though and his heart skipped at the realization that he was finally about to.

With one last glance at his perfectly coifed hair, Allard took a steadying breath and nodded to Sten, allowing his manservant to lead him to the hall where they would be wed officially.

Allard had offered to have an elven wedding but sitting before the elven council for their blessing was something that Fenian had refused to do. He was understandably still angry with them. Instead, he'd embraced life in the human kingdom, going out of his way to win over Allard's parents, taking on more duties than he needed to, and somehow, becoming the face of the elves to the humans.

And to Allard, he had become *everything*.

If there was such a thing as fate, Allard didn't doubt that they had been meant to find one another. Why else had he been invited into the Elven Veil on the night before Fenian's scheduled execution? Why had Fenian quite accidentally fallen into piles of bonding powder that very same day?

Thoughts swirled in his mind from the last few months. They'd spent so much time together and had learned so much. Allard could not remember ever being so happy and he knew it was the simple things like waking next to Fenian each morning and seeing his beautiful smile, that did it.

Sten patted his shoulder and gave him a warm smile and then it was time for Allard to stand on the pew, behind the curtains that separated him and Fenian.

He stepped up onto it, glancing at the crowd nervously and seeing all his friends, old and new. Knights he had always known, princes Nikolai and Nemir, his oaf friends, who he was happy to have reconnected with over the past few months, and even the members of the elven council who watched stoically.

He smiled out at them before his gaze fell on his parents.

They had adjusted remarkably well to Fenian's presence in their lives. As the wedding planning had progressed, his father had started to invite Fenian on strolls to discuss business, calling on his opinions more and more and going out of his way to simply chat. His mother had nearly lost her head trying to find a suitable wedding gift for him, settling on her grandmother's ring. Still, he was surprised to see the bright, encouraging smiles on each of their faces.

They had grown accustomed to Allard being with a male. The only other issue had been the matter of children. Perhaps, the recent announcement of their decision to adopt had been the last thing needed to fully smooth things over between them all.

Allard hoped so because little Liamar would need kind grandparents to help with the transition into human society.

Life had changed so much already that excitement and nerves bloomed in Allard's chest as he turned again to face the curtains separating himself and Fenian.

Finally, they swished apart with a dramatic flourish and Allard was face to face with the man of his dreams.

Fenian was stunning, as always, but in the human suit, cut and tailored so perfectly to fit his form, he was breathtaking. He did indeed match Allard, as the seamstress had said, but instead of silver thread, blue had been used in the stitching and embroidery, making the blue in his hair and eyes pop. His hair was braided half-up, the rest hanging down around his shoulders, exposing his handsome face, so full of emotions when he saw Allard.

They slowly walked forward and took each

other's hands, gazes never faltering as the occasions minister began his long, dry speech about their union.

How did I ever get so lucky? Fenian asked silently, smiling gently, his thumb stroking Allard's knuckles.

It was fate, Allard replied.

"Will you, Prince Allard, before the people of Tasnia, hold Fenian in your heart for the rest of your days?"

Allard smiled. He had been so eager to say these two small words.

"I will."

"Will you Fenian, before the people of Tasnia, hold Allard in your heart for the rest of your days?"

"I will."

Even though he'd known that those would be Fenian's words, his stomach still fluttered with delight.

"I officially declare you husbands. You may now kiss and seal the marriage."

Sparks flew when their lips met. It was the same every time. Despite being together for months already, despite sharing a bed and regularly making love, each kiss felt like that first one; exciting and full of promise.

Whatever changes were in store, he was ready to face it all with his love, his heart, his husband.

EPILOGUE

FENIAN

enian sat in the royal gardens, enjoying the gentle breeze moving through his hair and his child, sitting in his lap, absently twisting the ring on his finger thoughtfully.

"What happened to your parents?" Liamar suddenly asked, his large silver eyes looking up at him.

"My father had an accident at work. His boat sank and I lost both of my parents."

"And you went to the orphanage?"

"That's right."

"Did anyone ever adopt you?"

He shook his head.

Since collecting his new son from the orphanage

a few weeks ago, the small child had asked for the story over and over again, and Fenian always took the time to tell it because he knew it made Liamar feel less alone.

Liamar's small hands gripped the front of Fenian's shirt tightly and he sniffled.

Surprised, Fenian tilted his little chin up to see the tears in his eyes.

"What's wrong?" he asked gently.

"That's sad," Liamar said.

Fenian smiled softly.

"Maybe," he agreed. "But if things hadn't worked out that way for me, I wouldn't be here right now, with you and Allard."

Liamar's eyes widened.

"Really?"

"Oh yes, all the sad things happened to bring me down the path that led right here. To you two, the family that I love so much."

Liamar gazed thoughtfully down, playing with Fenian's ring again. Perhaps he was wondering if his own sad moments were necessary to bring him here. Perhaps he was wondering if this was his happy ending. Fenian hoped so.

Since taking Liamar in, all he seemed to want in life was for the child's happiness. Becoming a parent was like having an insurmountable load of love dumped atop you. It was overwhelming and important and too beautiful to understand.

A hand landed on his shoulder, and he glanced up, surprised to see Allard standing over him.

They smiled warmly at each other.

"Your grandmother is waiting to take you to the lake," Allard said to his son and Liamar lurched up, sad story forgotten, searching around anxiously.

"Don't worry, she won't leave without you. But she's already waiting for you. Let's go."

"Okay!"

Liamar dove from Fenian's lap and grabbed Allard by the hand, practically dragging him back toward the castle.

Laughing, Allard allowed it. Fenian stood and followed, chuckling when Allard suddenly yelled *"Run!"* and they began racing down the path, hand in hand.

He followed at a more reasonable rate, enjoying the scene, watching as Allard kissed the top of Liamar's head and lifted him into the carriage with his mother who immediately started chatting animatedly to Liamar.

He could hear her excited voice and his smile turned into a grin.

Both grandparents had completely blossomed once a grandchild had been brought into the mix.

Although he and the king were now on very good terms, it was still a shock to see him spin Liamar around in circles and offer him the candies he now kept in his pockets.

By the time the carriage was leaving, he reached his husband, wrapping an arm around his waist from behind as they watched it depart.

Allard immediately leaned back against him.

For a long moment, they stood like that, simply enjoying each other's presence.

"This is our first day without any obligations since we got Liamar," Fenian reminded Allard. "We should do something together."

"Hm… Would you like to go into town?"

Fenian bit his lip. He loved the human city, the *hustle, and bustle*, as Allard said, but Liamar hadn't seen it yet.

"Maybe not. I would feel guilty going without Liamar."

Allard chuckled.

"I should have known you would be such an amazing parent."

"You keep saying that."

"I know. I suppose it just amazes me."

Fenian's smile dropped into a frown.

"Why?"

Allard didn't answer and Fenian frowned,

suddenly understanding.

"You're amazed I'm a good parent since I never had any, is that what you mean?"

Allard sighed.

"Well, yes, but you make it sound worse than how I mean it."

He glanced at Fenian over his shoulder.

"It's just that…"

He swallowed and to Fenian's surprise, seemed unable to speak for a moment as emotion overwhelmed him.

With a deep breath, Allard finally forced the words out through inner speak.

You never had any kindness or love, yet you have so much to give…

Fenian blinked, his heart squeezing at the truth of that statement.

This time, he was the one that couldn't speak. He didn't know what to say until Allard turned in his arms, kissing him softly.

"Don't worry," he whispered. "I'll make up for all of the love you missed out on."

Finally, Fenian found his voice.

"You already have."

END

AFTERWORD

Thank you so much for reading The Elf's Prince! I absolutely adored getting to know these two. Seeing them, Fenian in particular, become worthy of love was so satisfying for me. I hope you loved them too!

If you enjoyed this book, please leave a review and check out the third book, The Wolf's Prince!

You can also get this high fantasy mm romance, The Prince and the Knight, for free by joining my newsletter at this link: https://storyoriginapp.com/giveaways/21c3f710-bd43-11ed-91d8-abb71c95245e

The Wolf's Prince BLURB:

THE PRINCE

Prince Nikolai isn't used to following the rules. As the youngest child, he has lived life with few responsibilities and plenty of adventure. But when a party leads to a romp in the gardens with a handsome shifter, Nikolai may have bitten off more than he can chew. What he thought was one night of wild fun may mean much more than he's prepared to give.

THE WOLF

Soren attended the human ball grudgingly as a show of goodwill. As the next in line to be pack alpha, he was chosen to be their representative. He expected it to be an unpleasant affair, but instead, he found his *fated mate*. Prince Nikolai is wild, fun, and full of passion. But he is also non-committal and criminally irresponsible.

It's not entirely a surprise when Nikolai runs after their bond has been made. But Soren needs more than a mate who he has to chase. Can Nikolai prove that he is worthy enough to be at his alpha's side? And can their bond become more than either could have longed for?

The Wolf's Prince is a fantasy adventure featuring a passionate wolf shifter with the world on his

shoulders, a flighty prince who thinks he can hide from his problems, and an unbreakable mating bond...

Read this exciting M/M adventure now.

Unsure? Please enjoy this preview!

THE WOLF'S PRINCE

CHAPTER ONE

NIKOLAI

Prince Nikolai stepped into the ballroom, grinning.

Human-like beings towered over the rest of the crowd, dressed in garb that the average gentlemen would find scandalous. Others were draped in fabrics and jewels in colors the likes of which he had never seen before, accented by pointed ears and vibrantly colored hair. There were humans too. They were just as easy to pick out. Like Nikolai, they were looking around in wonder at the variety of beings, all in one room for the first time.

Nikolai knew of the magical beings of their lands, but Casetro was a smaller country and they were limited to those that lived in the mountains, and in the ocean. Here in Tasnia, they were overrun by elves, oves, and even shapeshifters...

"Wow," Andrey breathed at his side.

Glancing up at his older brother, Nikolai took in the look of awe and trepidation on his charming face.

If not for the somber expression he carried permanently, Andrey would have been *very* pretty with his gentle features and sandy-colored hair. But because of his anxious disposition, Nikolai took the honor of cutest face in the family.

"Relax brother," he sighed. "Mingle with only the people you know. Then they'll introduce you to others if the moment is right. Look, there is King Jareth. He will be pleased to see you."

Andrey paled.

"Where are *you* going to be?"

"Dancing, of course!"

Andrey sighed and nodded, dismissing him, so Nikolai strode confidently into the room.

He loved a good party, and this one promised to be more fun than most.

Taking a glass of wine from a passing server, he drifted around the edges of the dance floor, watching the couples swirl to the orchestral music.

Quite notably, only humans were dancing. The

other races probably didn't know their dances. Well, all anyone needed was a good lead and Nikolai was an excellent one.

He tipped the rest of his drink back and turned, scanning the crowd.

Almost immediately, he caught eyes with a rather remarkable-looking elf. She was pale as moonlight and all of her hair was completely white. Her lashes were like snowflakes on her cheek, surrounding her pale gray eyes.

At her smile, Nikolai swept toward her, offering a hand and his trademark charming smile.

"Care to dance?" he asked.

"I'm afraid I don't know how."

"That's all right," he insisted. "I'll show you."

That seemed to be enough to convince her and she allowed him to lead her into the middle of the floor.

"It's quite simple for the ladies, all you have to do is allow me to move you around," he said with a wink.

She laughed.

"Very well, I won't fight you."

At her word, Nikolai began to move, moving slowly at first until she began to fall into the movements. Soon enough, we were swinging around the dance floor laughing because Nikolai kept going faster and faster to see how much she could handle.

"Are you trying to test me?" she demanded, grinning wide.

"Not at all," he argued.

"I may not know the human dances," she said, "but I believe we're supposed to at least keep beat with the music."

Chuckling, he slowed down their pace.

"I'm sorry, I couldn't help myself."

"Come, let us get a drink. I'll introduce you to some of my friends."

Mirra turned out to be her name and true to her word, she walked me around the party, introducing me to the other elves.

Aside from Mirra, they all appeared to be like the worst parts of the human aristocracy. Extremely formal, uptight, cunning, *boring*. Andrey would probably love them.

After speaking to a dull green-haired elf by the name of Seneca for far too long, Nikolai tugged Mirra away the moment he was distracted by someone else.

"Let's get that drink," he said as an excuse.

"Are you the *only* interesting elf?" he asked the moment they were out of earshot.

She laughed.

"In our defense, this is our first time mingling with humans like this. I think everyone is on edge, deciphering what is to come next."

"Tell me, how did you all come to be invited? I must ask Prince Allard what the reasoning for this was."

"You know him?"

"Oh yes, he's a friend. Us royals of the area have a way of sticking together." Nikolai snorted. "It can be quite annoying, but Allard isn't bad. A bit closed-minded, perhaps, but kind, really."

"Oh, you know Prince Allard too?"

At the sound of a deep, masculine voice, he turned and looked up—and then up some more—at the extremely tall and handsome *oaf* who stood behind him. He had vibrant red hair and was muscular with beautiful, tanned skin, almost all of it on display under thin strips of what Nikolai gathered to be a garment.

"Well, hello," he managed.

Nikolai wasn't exactly tall, to begin with. Most of the time he was lucky to stand higher than the average woman, but he more than made up for that with his face and body. In this case, it would have made no difference. He was sure that everyone looked quite the same from the oaf's vantage.

Suddenly, an identical oaf slid up next to the first.

Like the elves, the oves had long silky hair that they styled with braids. Where the elves favored jewels, the oves seemed to favor stones and bones. That didn't take away from their striking beauty though.

"I am Nikolai," he said, and then, because he didn't know what else to do, offered a hand.

"I am Tuboy, this is my twin brother Memet."

They took turns shaking Nikolai's hand, seeming to take effort not to squeeze too tightly. Mirra received a nod and a smile but did not return it.

"Excuse me," she muttered.

Nikolai watched her go, surprised. He'd once heard that elves didn't care for their half-brethren. The oves were half-ogre and apparently that was enough reason to disassociate. He didn't see the problem though. Aside from being large, they didn't appear much different from the elves.

And he'd thought Mirra would be a fun new friend…

Shaking the disappointment away, he turned back to the oaf twins who seemed unbothered by her reaction to them.

"So, you're friends of Prince Allard's?"

"Oh yes," Memet said warmly. "We got to know each other quite well when our brother Soluc first bonded with Prince Nemir."

Nikolai remembered finding that particularly hilarious at the time. The prince from Suvahl had accidentally entered into an unbreakable marriage union with a male oaf. Even now that made him grin with glee. Suvahl and Tasnia were both known for being closed-minded countries. They frowned upon same-sex partners. Add to that the non-human mate and it was downright ironic.

"I had never seen an oaf before, so I found that story hard to wrap my head around," Nikolai admitted, grinning.

They both chuckled, exchanging an amused look.

"Yes, well Nemir *is* quite tiny," Memet said. "But they make it work."

"I'm sure they do," Nikolai mused, following their gazes.

There at the back of the room, he spotted Prince Nemir, looking lovely with his dark curls hanging around his face, his hand linked with another large, redheaded oaf who seemed to be even bigger than his brothers.

Nikolai raised an incredulous brow.

"Prince Nemir never showed interest in men before. It hardly seems fair that he should up with such a *big* one…"

Memet snorted.

"Do you feel left out?" he teased. "That could easily be remedied."

Nikolai laughed, looking up at him with interest, then at Tuboy.

"Is this a two-for-one offer?" he asked boldly, feeling his cheeks heat at the suddenly flirtatious turn in the conversation.

They both grinned. Interest glinting in their eyes.

Perhaps the oves would be the most fun part of the party.

A prickling heat suddenly burned Nikolai's neck, drawing his attention away. He glanced over his shoulder and froze.

A breathtakingly beautiful man was *glaring* at him from only a couple of feet away, as though he had been personally offended by Nikolai. No human eyes caught the light like that, like a wild, dangerous animal and Nikolai couldn't move under his scrutiny. Even without the glint in his eyes, they were quite striking. Narrow, slanted, and intense.

"What are you?" Nikolai blurted by way of introduction.

The man blinked, his eyes suddenly dark as midnight on the new moon. He was a magnificent specimen, tall, broad, muscular, decked in earth-toned leather with fur accents all over.

All of these beings were stunning in their own

unique ways. But this one, his intensity, and focus made it impossible to look away.

"Have you never seen a shifter before?" he finally asked, still seeming annoyed by Nikolai.

"Well, I wouldn't know, would I?" Nikolai joked.

The shifter's lips didn't even twitch.

"Do you throw yourself at everyone with a hard cock to offer you?" he asked.

Nikolai's lips parted in surprise, his brows shooting up. He was so surprised that he had to bite his lip to stop himself from laughing out loud.

Finally, a snort burst free.

He glanced back at the oves, just remembering them. Luckily, at some point, they had been pulled into a conversation with someone else.

Turning back to the shifter, he shrugged sheepishly.

"We were just playing," he said. "That doesn't mean we would end up in bed together."

This didn't seem to mollify his new companion.

Nikolai spent a moment admiring him, while he wondered about his mood. His hair was long, silky straight, and jet black, his features masculine and sharp, with those piercing eyes and soft-looking pink lips.

"I would have tried my luck with you had I seen you first," Nikolai divulged.

He wasn't sure if jealousy was the reason for the shifter's hostility but he hoped it was.

To his delight, the anger faded from the shifter's face. Suddenly, he watched Nikolai as though unsure of what to make of him.

"I am Nikolai," he said, offering his hand.

The shifter took it.

"Soren," he said in a low voice.

Nikolai found himself holding Soren's hand for too long, feeling the warmth of his grip as fireworks erupted in his chest.

"Can you turn into anything you like?" he asked.

That finally drew a smile.

Soren shook his head.

"No."

A man of few words it seemed. That suited Nikolai just fine. The things he wanted to do with the shifter had little to do with talking anyway.

He bit his lip.

"Then what do you transform into? Will you show me?"

Soren tilted his head, considering.

"Perhaps… if you can guess."

Nikolai's lips tilted into a smile. He loved men who played games. It made everything more fun.

"Let me see," he said coyly, using the excuse to

step closer. "Hm, you're dressed well, but in so many layers. This fur collar..."

Nikolai allowed himself to touch Soren's broad shoulders, feeling the muscles under thick fur as he walked around Soren under the guise of examining his outfit.

"What about it?" Soren asked, turning his face to meet Nikolai's eyes as he came back around to the front of him.

There was amusement in his hooded eyes. And *interest.*

"It suggests that you are a hunter," Nikolai said, lowering his voice. "Perhaps you turn into a predator of the wilderness in the dark of the night?"

"Like a monster?" Soren asked, his voice suddenly husky, eyes glinting on Nikolai's.

"No," he whispered. "But perhaps... like a wolf?"

Suddenly, someone bumped into his back, sending him lurching forward.

Soren caught him, his hands firm and strong, holding Nikolai longer than necessary as he swiveled, in turn catching the man who'd lost his step.

"Careful there, friend," he said, catching the man's shoulders as he stumbled.

Nikolai was surprised to realize that it was Prince Allard, looking dashing as usual, in a fancy white suit accented with gold and blue to bring out his pale blond hair and grey eyes. His worried eyes widened in surprise when their gazes met.

"Prince Nikolai! You're here too?"

"Of course! Everyone is!" Nikolai laughed.

Nikolai had been looking forward to talking to him since receiving the invite, but now that Allard was here, he would have to get the short version of Nikolai's commendations. His mind was fixated on the shifter standing behind him with a firm grip still surreptitiously on Nikolai's hip, burning through his suit.

"What a revolutionary moment! I commend you and your family for choosing to bring the creatures of the wood to light. Such a daring idea," he grinned, patting him on the shoulder.

Allard shrugged helplessly, seeming distracted as well.

"Uh... yes."

He looked around, as though still unable to wrap his head around his own party. Perhaps it was shocking to see so many creatures mingling in one's own ballroom. Nikolai wouldn't know, but he was thrilled by it.

"Have you met Soren?" Nikolai asked, catching his sharp dark gaze as he glanced over his shoulder. "He's an actual shapeshifter!"

Before Allard could reply, his mother approached, smiling at Nikolai and placing a delicate hand on her son's elbow.

"There you are, dear. I was looking for you."

"I was about to do the same," Allard informed her. "May we speak in private?"

"Of course."

He waved to Prince Nikolai as she led him quietly from the hall into one of the adjoining chambers.

"Hm. Prince Allard is normally quite decorous. I'm surprised he didn't even acknowledge you," Nikolai said, feeling a little awkward on behalf of his new acquaintance. Even his mother had been tense, and the queen was normally quite fond of Nikolai.

"He was distracted," Soren said, sounding unbothered. "As was I."

Nikolai shivered as the hand on his hip slipped up to his waist.

"Ah yes, I believe you were about to show me your wolf form?"

Soren grinned an altogether feral expression on that handsome face with incisors too long to be human.

"I don't believe I said you were correct."

He tilted his head, another predatory expression, like he was watching Nikolai's every flickering move. It took his breath away. His heart started to pound.

"I have an idea," Soren said in a low tone. "How about you show me your form first? Then I'll show you mine."

Nikolai had to bite his lip to hold in a moan.

"Oh I can do that," he promised, blood rushing to fill his cock. "Quickly."

Soren's gaze darkened.

"Where?" he breathed.

Nikolai had a room here at the castle for the duration of his stay, but it was a shared suite with his brother so that wouldn't do. He was sure Soren had one too. They weren't going there either though, because Nikolai already had an erection working fast to tent the front of his trousers and he wasn't about to sift through an entire ballroom of people with that on display.

Instead, he glanced around, finding one of the wide balcony doors open to allow the spring air to flow within.

"Come," he said under his breath.

Avoiding meeting anyone's gaze, he darted through the crowd, hoping he was going unnoticed at the same time that he prayed to all the gods above that Soren was following.

He emerged into the cool night air and saw that

the darkness of the night was interrupted only by the candles that led to the garden.

The moment he swiveled around to see if Soren was coming, or if he'd run out here alone like a fool, the shifter was there, catching Nikolai in his arms.

Nikolai took a startled breath, realizing how close he had been followed.

"You should never just run like that from a predator," Soren hissed. "Don't you know a predator can't help but chase?"

Nikolai let out the breath he'd been holding, feeling the way his heart raced.

With the light from the ballroom behind him, Soren was a menacing halo and Nikolai wanted badly to be devoured.

"That's what I'd been hoping for," he whispered.

At that, Soren yanked him against his hard chest, making Nikolai grunt as Soren's lips closed over his.

They were barely through the doorway, hardly hidden at all, but as he felt the hungry taste of his mouth, Nikolai found what little bit of decency he possessed vanished.

Nikolai's arms came around his back, his hands just as hungry as his lips, feeling Soren's masculine frame. Such broad shoulders, a narrow waist, and hips cut out of marble that he couldn't help but grab onto.

Soren's mouth was like fire, white-hot kisses seared Nikolai's lips like he'd been wanting Nikolai forever and was desperate for him.

His tongue sent electric tendrils of pleasure shooting through Nikolai, practically making his hips buck.

Altogether too close for comfort, someone giggled, and Nikolai broke away with a gasp, swinging around to see a couple watching from behind the hanging drapes.

Soren's eyes were glowing silver like moonlight as he leaned toward Nikolai again. He truly looked like a wolf at that moment, about to devour Nikolai, very much like they had been joking—like Nikolai had *thought* they had been joking.

He swallowed, leaning away.

"Let's go for a walk," Nikolai said, clearing his throat. Might as well *pretend* they were going to be decent. Even if it was obvious they wouldn't be.

He took Soren's hand firmly in his own, leading him down the narrow steps, following the candles to the gardens.

He was already searching out hedges and trees, his gaze scanning what he could see in the dark shamelessly.

"This way," Soren whispered, and Nikolai realized that he could see better than him. Those eyes, he realized, must be for more than just show.

Gripping Nikolai's hand in his, he led him away from the candle-lit path until they were surrounded by darkness. Nikolai's heart was racing with anticipation.

"I'd been hoping to meet someone exciting tonight," Nikolai said as Soren pulled him into his strong embrace, letting out a low moan.

"You are so naughty," he growled.

Nikolai chuckled breathlessly.

"Let me show you how naughty I can be," he suggested.

In the dark, he reached down, feeling the long length of Soren's hard cock, his breath hitching at the size.

Soren groaned and with a sudden movement Nikolai couldn't predict, he was flat on his back on soft earth with his hands pressed over his head.

For a moment Nikolai wriggled but Soren only held him down tighter, pressing his hips against Nikolai's, grinding their erections together.

Nikolai stilled, letting Soren thrust against him while his head fell back.

"Oh… I was going to tell you not to mess up my clothes, but I think it's too late for that," Nikolai gasped.

"Forget your clothes. They're not important."

In demonstration, he gripped the front of Nikolai's suit, tearing it open.

Nikolai wasn't sure if he should be upset or aroused. His body chose the latter.

Soren's unforgiving grip moved to Nikolai's exposed skin. The chilly night air had made his nipples pebble and Soren wasted no time rubbing the hard nubs with his thumbs, a deep growl reverberating through his chest.

Trembling, Nikolai reached up, blindly feeling Soren through all his clothes.

"Not fair," he mumbled, but Soren did not seem in a hurry to match Nikolai's level of undress.

Instead, he allowed his hands to drift down even further, to the edges of Nikolai's trousers which he then slid deft fingers within.

Nikolai gasped at the brush of fingertips on his damp tip.

Another finger pressed between his parted lips and he sucked it at once, relishing in the deep moan it elicited.

"You're gorgeous," Soren breathed.

Nikolai paused, eyes widening as he realized that Soren could see him.

"Now that's *really* not fair," he said around

Soren's finger. "We should go inside. I want to see you too."

His first time bedding someone who wasn't human and he couldn't even see the beast. Calling him that, even in his head, made a shiver travel Nikolai's body. He truly was about to have sex with someone who was part animal and that thrilled him to the core.

"No. This is better. Here under the moonlight, as is natural."

Nikolai hadn't even noticed the moon. It was shrouded in clouds and he had been distracted. Now that he searched for the pale glow of dim light in the sky, he could see it, but it wasn't an obvious presence.

Perhaps to Soren's instincts, it was impossible to ignore.

Soren pulled back and there was the sound of fabric rustling.

Nikolai reached out eagerly, his hands meeting soft skin, hard muscles, and course chest hair.

He let out an appreciative moan, letting his hands skate over the defined chest and stomach, lowering until he reached what he had been seeking.

Soren's length was out, exposed to the air and straining toward Nikolai's touch and it was *big*.

He bit his lips, letting his fingers fun down the

full length of it, moaning at the thought of taking it all within him. He closed his hands around Soren's length.

"So you approve?" Soren asked gruffly, remaining still while Nikolai examined him.

"Oh yes," he breathed. "I made a good choice tonight. I want you inside me."

Soren let out a low inhuman growl at Nikolai's words and suddenly, he was off him, yanking Nikolai's trousers down.

Nikolai struggled to help kick them free, managing to get his boots off and probably scuffing them beyond repair without care before he was completely nude, and Soren finally climbed atop him.

Their naked flesh met, an electric touch of skin that seemed to tingle the nerve endings in Nikolai's entire body.

He shuddered, spreading his legs, pressing up to grind against the large cock he'd so recently held in his hands.

Soren moaned and his lips pressed down against Nikolai's again, ravishing him with hot passion the likes of which Nikolai wasn't sure he had ever felt.

Nikolai was clutching the shifter's back, nails digging into his flesh, ready to come from the thrill of it and they had barely started.

"Soren," he groaned. "Fuck me. Please. Quickly."

Soren's entire body shuddered.

He reached between them, his fingers finding Nikolai's soft entrance. For a moment, he felt him there, his kiss slowing while he explored.

"Would you really have let those big oaf cocks into this tight little hole?" he growled.

Nikolai let out a breathy chuckle.

"What can I say, I like a big boy."

"I can give you that."

"Yes," Nikolai groaned. "Stop teasing and give it to me."

Suddenly, Soren moved down, lowering himself and without warning, sucking his cock almost fully into his mouth.

Nikolai arched off the cold ground instinctively. His fingers tangled into Soren's silky hair. For a moment, he almost pulled his sleek wet heat down to further bury his cock down the other man's throat, then at the last second, he shoved Soren off.

"I want to come with your cock inside me," he gasped. "Not in your mouth."

Soren moaned in response, slipping lower, putting his mouth to other uses.

Nikolai's eyes rolled.

He loved having a hot wet tongue against his hole and so few people did it, especially on a one-night fling.

Steadying his breath, Nikolai pulled his knees up, allowing better access.

Soren wasn't shy either. He gripped Nikolai's cheeks, holding them apart, and started to thrust his tongue within him, not stopping until Nikolai was shaking and mewling, his cock leaking. He knew he was completely shameless. If anyone caught them, his brother would be mortified. A prince wasn't supposed to get fucked out in the open, during a party, and with a total stranger. But it gave Nikolai a thrill.

"Deeper," he begged, and Soren drew up, positioning himself at once to give Nikolai what his body craved.

"Deep, and big," Soren whispered, pressing his tip to Nikolai's entrance. "Anything else?"

"Yes," Nikolai gasped. "Do it now."

"So demanding *and* impatient too," Soren mused, pressing his hips forward.

Nikolai cried out when Soren's tip breached his entrance. The pleasure of being stretched apart was intensified by Soren's generous girth.

His thighs trembled so hard he had to clutch his legs to his chest and force air into his lungs, trying to clear his head slightly so he wouldn't come immediately. He wanted to ride this out, no pun intended, to the very limit.

"Does it hurt?" Soren asked, sounding concerned.

Nikolai chuckled breathlessly.

"Do you want me to repeat the part about loving a big cock inside me?" he gasped. "Because I will. You feel incredible."

Soren released a breath he had been holding and slid in further.

Nikolai moaned loudly.

He clutched his knees, holding on for dear life as Soren started to thrust into him, long and deep, just like he wanted, pressing down at the end of each thrust and grinding in a little bit further.

He relaxed his weight onto Nikolai, folding him up even tighter and grinding deep.

"Like this?" he growled, and Nikolai could feel the reverberations through his body, that slightly inhuman sound again. He shuddered, head falling back as he cried out in pleasure.

Somehow, his hands found Soren's back, skating over the muscles, sleek with sweat, then tangling in his shockingly soft hair, then grabbing his ass and squeezing it hard, controlling the speed and angle that Soren fucked him while he completely lost himself.

When he started to come, Soren kept going,

gasping at the way his muscles tightened and flexed inside but unrelenting in his movements, and to Nikolai's delight, his orgasm stretched on, continuing in spurts. He would have a moment to breathe and then the wave began again, overwhelming pleasure washing through him.

Soren didn't stop, pressing him into the ground with the strength of his thrusts, clutching Nikolai's shoulders as he pounded into him, groaning in time with Nikolai's gasps of pleasure.

"Stop exposing your neck to me like that," Soren suddenly gasped. "It is too tempting to bite."

The idea of a shifter losing control on him, for this session of passion to become even more animalistic, was irresistible.

Nikolai tilted his head away even more.

"Do it," he gasped. "Bite me."

Soren let out a guttural growl and without any more hesitation, he lurched forward.

His teeth sank deep into Nikolai's neck, just above the collarbone, the angle of his cock shifting. Nikolai gasped. Soren's entire body jerked with pleasure. It was an explosion of pain and rapture unlike anything Nikolai had experienced before. Again, he came hard, barely registering the fact that Soren was coming inside him, filling him with his seed.

Everything faded to white hot pleasure.

When Nikolai slowly returned to his body, his toes were numb, and his ears were ringing. Soren had collapsed on top of him, gasping hard, his thick cock still buried deep within Nikolai's hole.

It took Nikolai a minute of lying there, feeling the air cooling his skin, and the brush of grass and dirt on his back, to find a voice. Still, it came out quiet and distant when he spoke.

"What is that?" he asked softly.

Soren pressed his hips down, letting Nikolai feel the extent of his cock and the thickening base.

"My knot," he whispered.

His lips pressed to the side of Nikolai's throat, just above the bite which now ached.

"Your knot?" he repeated, feeling the swollen member stretching him from within.

His eyes fluttered shut.

If he had any energy left, he would have tried to ride it.

As it were, he remained still, simply enjoying the pleasurable sensation without pushing it.

"So, you really are a wolf then," he whispered. "Or some type of canine."

"Wolf," Soren agreed gruffly. "And now you are an honorary one too."

"And all it took was hot sex?" Nikolai asked, smiling softly, his fingers tracing over Soren's cooling back. "I'm honored… Perhaps we can make me a wolf a couple more times before we leave. How long will your stay here be?"

"We leave tomorrow," Soren said, and he lifted himself onto his elbows to look down at Nikolai. "Of course, I will satisfy you over and over again. As much as you desire and more."

Nikolai shivered.

Despite himself, he clenched around Soren's swollen cock, making the shifter moan. He dipped down, pressing their lips together once more before lifting to look at Nikolai again.

Nikolai's eyes had finally adjusted to the night. He could see Soren's form over him, the beautiful curve of his muscular shoulders, a halo of blue moonlight on his black hair.

He reached up, touching the shifter's cheek, marveling at the silver sheen on his eyes as they fluttered shut.

"How does it feel?" Soren whispered. "To have found your lifemate?"

Lifemate?

Nikolai blinked.

In his experience, it normally took a couple of sessions of lovemaking for a man to think they were a serious item.

He smirked.

"Am I that good?" he teased. "You want it to be forever?"

"Of course," Soren agreed. "I wouldn't have given you the mating bite and my knot otherwise."

He lowered, pressing their lips together again, softly, *lovingly.*

When he lifted enough for their eyes to meet, Nikolai stared in confusion.

"I thought this night would be tedious," Soren whispered, fingers brushing Nikolai's smooth cheek. "Instead, I was blessed by Medeira and her moonlight to meet you, my Nikolai, my *mate.*"

To be continued in The Wolf's Prince

ABOUT THE AUTHOR

When not writing, Sienna Sway can be found planning countless books and entertaining plot bunnies.

She is the mother to a loving toddler and partner to a lovely Irish man. She also lives in beautiful Coquitlam, BC in Canada, surrounded by mountains and forests.

She doesn't know how she got so lucky but is so grateful to her family and readers for supporting her dreams. She hopes to pay it forward.

Thank you for being here!

Made in the USA
Las Vegas, NV
09 July 2023

74409570R00194